NANA MALONE
JAMIE POPE

A *Vow* of
SEDUCTION

HARLEQUIN® KIMANI™ ROMANCE

ISBN-13: 978-0-373-86465-2

A Vow of Seduction

Copyright © 2016 by Harlequin Books S.A.

The publisher acknowledges the copyright holders
of the individual works as follows:

Hot Night in the Hamptons
Copyright © 2016 by Nana Malone

Seduced Before Sunrise
Copyright © 2016 by Jamie Pope

PLEASE RECYCLE
THIS PRODUCT IS RECYCLABLE

Recycling programs
for this product may
not exist in your area.

HARLEQUIN®
www.Harlequin.com

Printed in U.S.A.

Hot Night in the Hamp

"You can do that? Pretend? That Saturday night never happened?"

She tilted her chin up. "Yeah, given your rep, I know you can."

His brows snapped down. And then before she knew it, his lips were on hers. Harsh and firm. His tongue delved into her mouth and demanded she respond. Traitor that her body was, she melted as if today was a continuation of Saturday night and Sunday morning. She knew that when it came to him, she was weak. She wouldn't be able to stop.

Gabe pulled back. "Still want to pretend we don't know each other?"

Seduced Before Sunrise

"I could really go for something sweet."

"Yeah," he said distractedly. "I could, too. There's just one thing I have to do first."

"What?"

He grabbed the edges of her towel and tugged on them until her body was pressed against his again. She looked up at him, curiosity in her eyes, but that changed when he inched his mouth closer to hers. He didn't want to steal a kiss. He didn't want to take her by surprise. He wanted her to know it was coming.

Nana Malone is a *USA TODAY* bestselling author. Her love of all things romance and adventure started with a tattered romantic suspense she borrowed from her cousin on a sultry summer afternoon in Ghana at a precocious thirteen years old. She's been in love with kick-butt heroines ever since. You'll find Nana working hard on additional books for her series. And if she's not working or hiding in the closet reading, she's acting out scenes for her husband, daughter and puppy in sunny San Diego.

Books by Nana Malone

Harlequin Kimani Romance

Wrapped in Red with Sherelle Green
Tonight with Sienna Mynx
A Vow of Seduction with Jamie Pope

Visit the Author Profile page at
Harlequin.com for more titles.

Jamie Pope first fell in love with romance when her mother placed a novel in her hands at the age of thirteen. She became addicted to love stories and has been writing them ever since. When she's not writing her next book you can find her shopping for shoes or binge watching shows on Netflix.

Books by Jamie Pope

Harlequin Kimani Romance

Surrender at Sunset
A Vow of Seduction with Nana Malone

Visit the Author Profile page at
Harlequin.com for more titles.

CONTENTS

To Fritz. Thank you for
making my New York Valentine's Day so fun.

Dear Reader,

Thank you so much for reading *Hot Night in the Hamptons*.
I was once a young PR intern many moons ago, so Elina
and Gabe were a fun little trip back in time. I may or may
not have drawn more than a little inspiration from my own
life. Shh, don't tell anyone.

I also loved that I got to revisit Delilah and Willow from
my Donovans series! Next up for me, I've got more
Donovans (yes, which means more Delilah) and many
more Kimani books. So sit back, relax and happy reading!

If you want to chat with me, I'm pretty easy to find!

Website: www.NanaMalone.com

Facebook: www.Facebook.com/NanaMaloneWriter

Twitter: www.Twitter.com/NanaMalone

Nana

HOT NIGHT
IN THE HAMPTONS

Nana Malone

Chapter 1

"You're headed off to your friend's wedding this weekend, right?"

Elina Sinclair barely managed to keep herself from groaning out loud to her boss. She hated weddings. Reece was the sole reason she was going. Her best friend had seen her through enough trauma in her life. The least she could do was be there for her girl as she walked down the marriage-guillotine-aisle. "Yeah, I leave tonight. I'll be back on Sunday. But if you need anything, don't hesitate to call."

Her boss, Delilah Donovan, leaned back against the sofa in the lounge area of their office. In the far corner, Delilah's business partner, Willow, hunched over her laptop.

"Honey, it's a wedding, *and* a couple of days off. Enjoy it. Flirt with the cute best man. That's what you're supposed to do."

Elina considered this. Maybe right now was *not* the time

to tell Delilah that she loathed every single thing about weddings. That, thanks to her mother, the fairy-tale luster had worn off…probably not a good idea to mention that since her boss had just tied the knot herself. "Yep, I hear you. Fun, fun. That's me." She forced a smile.

More like she'd rather be following some survival guide through the Mojave Desert, eating things gross enough to make her stomach turn, than go to this wedding. *It's for Reece.* Yeah, for her bestie, she could suck it up and put on her big-girl thong.

Delilah rolled her eyes. "Elina, I swear it's like you don't want the time off."

"Not really. I've gotten used to the pace, and I like it." D. Donovan Image Consultants was a boutique public relations agency. They cleaned up the reputation of the worst media screwups. Made problems go away. Technically they were PR firm meets law firm, but they were so much more than that. They affected real change in people's lives. Their clients included CEOs, diplomats, politicians and athletes. Delilah didn't handle celebrities anymore though, thanks to several bad apples.

After graduation, Elina had been drifting, looking for something permanent. Trying to decide if she was going to grad school or not, and she'd seen one of Delilah's clients on television with Delilah standing right next to him—clearly in charge of things. Elina had been fascinated and contacted the agency right away, practically begging for an interview. She'd even offered to work for free for a month. To her surprise, Delilah had said yes. During that month, Elina did everything from pick up dry cleaning for Delilah and her partner, Willow Green, to chasing down wayward clients and dragging them back to rehab, to drafting media statements. Delilah had hired her after that. That had been a year ago, and Elina wasn't looking back. She didn't know any of her friends who had that dynamic of a job. Especially not at twenty-three. And the best part was, Delilah was having a huge impact in the PR industry and she was only twenty-six. The story was she'd worked a great deal at Park & Associates where they paid for law school while she worked for them. So she'd gone to school at night, all the while getting hands-on experience from the best. Elina wanted to be her when she grew up.

"Speaking of you working your butt off, Willow and I wanted to talk to you about something."

The stunning redhead's alabaster skin looked like the center of an Oreo, where Elina and Delilah acted as the cookies. Willow smiled. "You've done some outstanding work and really stepped up in the last year. It doesn't matter what we ask of you, and that's really impressive."

Delilah added, "I think you're almost ready for your first solo client. Maybe we'll start with someone who doesn't have a huge profile to not overwhelm you. The next client I have coming in might be a pain, but I'll give you parts of the account for sure. We'll see how you do, then bump you up to do one all on your own. How does that sound?"

Elina giddily shifted in her seat like a kid on the last day of school. She tried to speak but all she could manage was a guppy impression. Finally, she found the words. "Oh my God, are you serious?"

Delilah nodded. "Yep. You've done great work. And you make things happen for yourself. You remind me of me."

"Thank you so much. I really appreciate it," Elina sputtered.

"You should celebrate and take off to the wedding early. Catch the off-peak jitney before everyone else heads to the Hamptons and it gets too crowded."

Willow unfolded her long limbs and stood up from the

bright pink lounger. The office decor was cool, comfy and contemporary with a mix of boho chic. Delilah had converted the warehouse space next to her old apartment into the offices for D. Donovan. When she'd married her husband, Nate, they'd moved to some fancy penthouse, and Willow had rented her old apartment from the couple.

As Elina walked back to her desk, she wanted to dance. Or laugh, or run and tell someone. *Except there's no one to tell.* There was her mother. And she had friends. *Good* friends, though none as good as Reece. But she hardly saw them, because she'd been so focused on her job for the last year. Well, it didn't matter that she had no one to call. Maybe Willow was right. She could head up now and spend some extra time with Reece...*before* the wedding. Inject some fun into her life.

And just like that, her happy mood evaporated. Maybe it wasn't too late to back out. *No.* She could support her best friend no matter how she personally felt about weddings. Even if it killed her...slowly...with a pickax to the soul.

Her phone buzzed in her pocket, and she pulled it out to answer. But when she saw it was her mother, she sent the call directly to voice mail. Elina knew her mother by now. It was her mother's third call that morning, which could only mean one thing.

Either she had some new boyfriend that she was desperate to introduce Elina to, *or*, she had a man for Elina. The last thing Elina needed was a guy in her life. She'd told her mother this countless times. Of course her mother didn't listen. The woman was always chasing love. Had been ever since Elina was little. Hell, she'd been married seven times. On paper, her mother was Gigi Meyers Sinclair James Adams Sinclair Thomas Stoya Sinclair.

Her parents had married three times. They just couldn't leave each other alone. No matter how destructive and codependent they were. Growing up, Elina must have been the only kid of divorced parents who wished her parents *wouldn't* get back together. She adored her father and could never understand why he put up with her mother's dramatics. Must have been love. After he died, her mother had been devastated, and Elina felt like part of her heart died, too. Her parents might not have been married at the time, but her mother always called her father her greatest love.

After seeing what love could do to her mother, and the pain of losing her father, Elina refused to let love do that to her again. No matter how hard her mother tried to change that.

Nope, Elina had a singular focus—her career. There would be no falling in and out of love, no series of walks down the aisle. She'd seen it all. And weddings, love and relationships held zero appeal. She'd keep her eyes on the prize—kicking butt and showing Delilah what she could do.

Chapter 2

Promises, promises. So what if Elina promised herself she'd never attend another wedding. She'd lied. At the time she never thought Reece would get married. But she would make it through this weekend. She *had* to.

Reece was waiting at the jitney stop with a convertible and a grin as the sun glinted through her golden locks. "Jesus, girl, could you be any more Hamptons?" Elina laughed as she strolled over to the car.

Reece was far more exuberant in her greeting. "Ohmygod, ohmygod, ohmygod. You're here, you're here!" The screeching was punctuated with a running launch and a huge hug. It was a good thing that Reece was all of five feet tall, otherwise she would have knocked Elina onto her butt.

Although Reece was small, she was mighty. The hug she gave was strong enough to cut off crucial air supply. Elina hugged her back, reveling in the familiar embrace.

When they'd been paired as freshman year roommates

in boarding school, Elina didn't think she and the blonde Southern transplant from Georgia would have anything in common. But from the moment Reece had barged into the dorm room, she'd been one of those friends who wouldn't let go. Reece was one of those people who left no option *but* to love her. And if you didn't love her at first, she was going to *make* you love her. The girl didn't take no for an answer. It was probably why the two of them got along so well.

"Honey, when I said I was coming early, I didn't mean for you to pick me up personally. I thought you'd send Uber or something."

Reece's delicate brow drew up. "You're kidding me, right? First of all, my mother-in-law and Mama have this thing on lock. All I have to do is show up. And I'm a happy bride for it, not having to make any decisions." She laughed. "All I wanted was final say on the dress and the hair and makeup, because you know Mama would have me looking like a pageant girl reject if I let her. Southern women and the big hair. I didn't give two flying figs about the whole Hamptons wedding nonsense. All I care about is Adam. So I have nothing to do except walk down the aisle."

And that was why Elina loved her bestie. Keeping it real and keeping it relaxed. Most women, like Elina's mother, would be in full bridezilla mode right about now.

Reece wrestled her bag from her and tossed it into the back of the car. "Gimme that."

"Seriously, Reece, I've got seven inches on you. I can carry my own bag."

"Look, I know how you feel about weddings, so I'm going to make this whole process as easy on you as possible."

"You don't have to do that. This is *your* day, or weekend rather."

"I'm so glad you feel that way, so you might as well shut up and do as I tell you."

Elina laughed. "Okay, suit yourself."

"I will, thank you very much. We're off to brunch."

"Seriously? There has to be some wedding thing to do."

"It is not my wedding *day*. I have nothing to do except hang with my girl. Not until tomorrow, anyway. This is the day *before* my wedding day. And I get to do what I want. We've already done the shower and the bachelorette party and everything, so we get to chill out. Come on, I'm starving."

That was the other thing about Reece. For such a small woman, she ate enough for two grown men. "Then by all means. Let's feed the tiny beast."

By the time they were seated in a lovely café overlooking the water, Reece had already regaled her with stories of wedding shenanigans from both her mother and her mother-in-law-to-be. The two women got along, but they were so eager to one-up each other, things had gotten more than a little crazy.

"I mean, you should see the damn centerpieces, Elli. They're huge. It'll be any wonder the guests can see around the things to chat. And don't even get me started on the gift bags. I mean who needs Tiffany's cell phone charms? Explain this to me. Who?"

"Your mother?" Elina laughed.

"God, that woman is infuriating. Speaking of infuriating, how is Mama Sinclair?"

Elina sighed. "I've gotten three calls from her today alone, with two 'call me' urgent texts."

"Maybe it's important. You know. She might need you."

She shook her head. "No. Since she has a habit of calling so often we established that if it was an emergency she needs to text 911, otherwise I'll call her when I get a chance." Elina shrugged. "And right now, I haven't had a chance."

Reece grinned. "Let me guess, you had to define what an actual emergency was at some point?"

Elina almost choked on her French fry she was laughing so hard. "It's like you were there."

"Nope, I just know your mother."

"I mean who else has to explain to their parents that what to wear on a date is *not* an emergency. Or some guy not calling is *not* an emergency. Or that some guy sexting a pic of his schlong is *not* an emergency. I finally had to outline an emergency as something that involved the fire department, police, ambulance, illness, hospitalization or impending death. And even then, she called me once because she pulled a muscle at boot camp and the paramedic who came to the park to check her out was super-cute. She claimed that required an ambulance so that was warranted." Elina shook her head. "This is my life."

Reece just laughed. "I love your mama, so awesome."

"That hurts me right here." Elina put a hand over her heart as she laughed.

"Enough Mama madness. How's the job?" Reece asked.

"Great, actually. I came early because Delilah gave me the rest of the day off." Elina filled Reece in on the details, and true to form Reece was genuinely happy for her.

They chatted for another half hour when Reece did a double take and beamed. "Look, there's Adam and Gabe."

Elina finished her fry and plastered a smile on her face. She had to go into happy wedding mode. Not that she had any problem with Adam. As a best-friend-in-law-to-be, he could have been worse. Adam was really sweet and loved her bestie, so he was okay in Elina's book. It was just the whole matrimony thing. Why couldn't they just be the Goldie Hawn and Kurt Russell of normal people?

"Hey, ladies. Fancy meeting you here." Adam kissed Reece on the nose. He and Reece were just about the cutest thing in the world to watch. Adam was maybe Elina's height if she was being generous. And his dark hair and eyes were the perfect contrast to Reece's golden hair and bright blue eyes. They were like a pocket-size Ken and Barbie.

Elina stood, and they enveloped each other in a huge hug. "Hey, stranger. You ready to make an honest woman out of my friend here?" she asked.

"She's making *me* the honest man." Adam beamed.

Elina shook her head. The two of them making googly eyes was not something an avowed single girl needed to see. She turned to Gabe, who gently released Reece from a hug. Or more like, Reece finally let him go.

Elina felt vindicated when she saw him gulp for air. "You must be Gabe. I've heard a lot about you." She thrust out her hand, but he ignored it. Instead, he wrapped her in a warm hug. The near physical slam of lust was enough to steal her breath and singe her panties.

He smelled like sandalwood and the beach, and she was so temporarily blindsided that she almost leaned in and inhaled. Gabe released her quickly and stumbled back.

When he spoke, his voice was husky. "Reece's mom says you don't shake hands with family. And seeing as we're family now, that calls for a hug."

It took her several seconds to find her voice. Where the hell had she misplaced that thing? She told herself it wasn't her fault. Any red-blooded woman would have this response to a guy like Gabe.

She judged him to be just a little over six feet. And while he was lean, he was solid. From what Elina could see from his biceps and forearms, he didn't skip time at the gym. And his soft cotton T-shirt didn't hide a thing.

Certainly not the defined pectorals. *Get it together, Elina. He's just a guy. You've seen them before.*

She managed to stammer, "Right, family." He hadn't been able to make it to the shower, and somehow through the years they'd never met. Because if she had met him, she'd have prepared herself for that stunning lopsided smile. Maybe she would have done some mental calisthenics or something. His eyes were a beautiful shade of green—so clear and alert, with flecks of blue and brown and yellow. Butterflies danced low in her belly, and her smile broke free even though she knew better. Her body—tingling. Brain—on vacation. His mouth was moving. Damn, what was he saying? *Focus.*

"Really glad you could make it down early. Now we can get to know each other before the big day." He was flirtatious, and his voice held a hint of mischief. And he stunned Elina into a momentary silence.

Yes, hell yes. Wait, what? *No.* No. She was not looking for anything. The *last* thing she needed was a guy. Particularly *this* guy, who was too good-looking for his own good.

Besides, she'd had someone like this once. Beautiful to look at, charming as hell. She'd even considered forever with him, too. That is, until she discovered he was just as charming with several other girls. No. She knew better than to get sucked in.

"Yep. Well, I wanted to get some extra time in with Reece."

"I think Reece will probably be busy, but I'm sure we can probably find a few things to get up to in the Hamptons. Let me be your guide." He was persistent.

Oh boy. This guy would guide her right into trouble. The naked, fun kind. But trouble nonetheless. "Somehow, I have a feeling that you might be the kind of guide that gets me lost."

He winked at her. "Isn't that half the fun?"

Elina was sure of one thing. If she wanted to hold on to her panties and her sanity, she had to stay on her toes around Gabe. It didn't matter if he made her insides go all fluttery. Besides, if she ever wanted her own solo client, then she had to keep her eyes on the prize and not on his muscles.

It was the chase. It had to be the chase. Gabe Alexander stared at Elina on the dance floor. She was laughing at something that Reece's mom said and he was completely struck by her. Had been since yesterday. But no amount of charm and wit was getting through to her. She was like flirting with a brick wall.

Normally, women fell into his lap. He wasn't used to doing so much work to get someone's attention. But it didn't matter what he did, Elina gave him nothing to work with. He already knew from Reece and Adam that she didn't have a boyfriend. No recent breakups. She was single.

And he felt that electric current when they first hugged, so she was attracted, but she still didn't take the bait.

Not like he had time to chase a girl right now. He was chasing funding for his first movie, and was running out of time. *Stone Heart* was the unofficial biography of his grandmother, Gretta Stone, and how she became the first Hollywood movie executive back in the fifties. She was the reason his father got a start in the business.

He'd wanted to tell the story for a long time, but the funding was difficult. *Well, it doesn't have to be difficult.* But there was no way he was asking his father for the funds. That was the last place he wanted to go. Not that the old man would even back the film. Once he'd transitioned out of acting, he'd become a director, only focusing on the big-money projects. He didn't think the movie would make him any money.

It didn't matter, though; Gabe was determined to do this on his own. For once, he wanted his career to be his own with no influence from the old man. He owed his grandmother everything. Between her and his mother, they'd pulled him back from the brink. He was getting this story told.

As a kid, it made sense. He was Andrew Alexander's son. It made logical sense to follow in his father's footsteps. But soon, all anyone had ever seen when he walked into a room was his father. So, like any teenager, he'd rebelled. And he was still paying for that rebellion.

But he had a few friends in the business, and plenty of money, thanks to a wildly popular trilogy he did when he was twelve, but he didn't have *producer* money. And the rest of the world saw him as that spoiled kid, acting out, boozing it up and sleeping with too many women.

Thanks to his grandmother, after college, he'd long since cleaned up his act, even made some wise investments. He needed to change that bad-boy image if he wanted a career in this business.

But even with everything going on, and everything on the line, he was completely drawn to Elina. It was mostly her laugh. Every time she talked to Reece she was happy and giddy. They laughed like two teenage girls snickering over some boy they liked.

But during the ceremony, Elina looked haunted, scared. He wanted to know why. More than that, he wanted to fix it. To make it go away.

"You stare any harder at her and I will make you declare your intentions."

Gabe laughed and slapped Adam on the back. "How is the newly minted groom doing?"

His best friend grinned. "I'm perfect. I can't believe it's finally done. She's mine."

Watching Adam and Reece almost made Gabe want to settle down. They were so suited to each other, and really happy. "Good for you, man. I'm happy for you. And I hope you enjoy your wedding present to the fullest."

Adam shook his head. "You didn't need to lend us your yacht. You know that, right?"

"Whatever. It just sits most of the time. Someone deserving might as well get use out of it." His father had bought the yacht and signed him as a co-owner, insisting it was a good investment and good for the image, but the old man never went near the thing. He hated the water.

"Well, we appreciate it nonetheless." Adam inclined his head toward Elina. The photographer was shooting her in the dimming sunlight. "So what's the word, man? Are you going to make a move or what?"

Gabe rolled his eyes. "Are you kidding me? I've been putting on all my best moves since yesterday. This is my game. It's the only game I've got."

Adam laughed. "Man, you're going to need to work on that. That pretty mug will only take you so far."

Gabe stroked his chin. "Don't be jealous. Only one of us can be pretty."

Adam rolled his eyes. "I'll settle for being the smart one, then. Look, dude, if you want to get closer to Elina, you can't spit game at her. You have to talk to her. Be real. She's pretty cool."

Gabe cocked his head and studied her. "What's her problem with weddings, anyway?"

Adam stared into his scotch glass. "Problem? What problem?"

"Oh, come on. You can see it, too. She looks uncomfortable, unhappy even."

"Okay, but you didn't hear this from me. Her mother has been married seven times. It soured her on the whole marriage thing."

Gabe whistled low. "Seven?"

"Yeah, a couple of times to Elina's dad, but it never seems to work out. So Elina has a *thing* about weddings."

That would certainly explain it. "I get you."

Adam shoved him in the arm. "What are you sniffing after Elina for, anyway? Don't you have your hands full?"

Gabe finished his drink. "Yeah, I've got a few things going on, but that doesn't mean I can't appreciate a beautiful woman."

"Between the funding hunt, the movie and casting, how will you find the time?"

"You just let me worry about that. I've got the funding under control. Well, mostly anyway. I'm meeting with that fixer in the city on Monday. She's got a lot of experience with entertainment clients. She'll help me change my image as well as get some studio appointments. She's a pretty big player and can help get some buzz around my name."

"That's great." Adam studied his glass again. "Here's the thing, Gabe. As the best-friend-in-law, I have to warn you, Elina's not that girl that you screw around with and leave. Reece will have your rear if you break her heart. She's very protective of Elina."

"Would you relax? I have everything under control. I'm not going to hurt her." He shrugged. "I just want to see her smile." And that was mostly true.

Chapter 3

Water, water, everywhere, and no way to swim to shore. At least not in her dress. Reece had left out one specific detail to Elina. She hadn't mentioned the damn reception was on a yacht. With no way out, except to swim. And in the slinky vermilion-red mermaid-style gown, there was no way that was happening.

Elina grabbed a glass of champagne from a passing tray. If there was no getting off the boat, she might as well have a drink…or several. She searched the crowd for someone to talk to other than Adam's spoiled, moneyed, Wall Street friends.

"You want to tell me why you're all alone drinking away your sorrows?"

Elina smirked before turning around to face Gabe. God, the man was sexy. It really was unfair. The whole effect of movie-star-gorgeous looks was exacerbated by the impeccable Tom Ford tuxedo. She had to hand it to the man, he was wearing that tux.

"I'm not sad." She lied, "I'm celebrating. Like everyone else."

Gabe shook his head, the corners of his lips tipped up in a ghost of a smile. "Usually, happy comes with a lot more smiles."

Elina forced her lips to turn up. "See, happy."

"Okay, you got me wrong," he said, laughing.

She tried to change the subject. "What about you? Why are you over here keeping sorrowful me occupied? You could be up there dancing with the two bridesmaids who have been eyeing you all night."

Gabe never took his eyes off of her. "Maybe it's because the girl I want to dance with is drinking by herself."

Elina put up a hand. "Can we just stop with the whole flirtation thing? I mean, obviously you're beautiful, but you're barking up the wrong tree."

Gabe nodded thoughtfully. "Oh, I see. You're not into guys?"

Elina sputtered and laughed. "I am. I'm just not into guys *right now.* All your best efforts in the last two days are being wasted on me, when you could be using them on ready-to-ride bridesmaids."

He shrugged. "I think I'll stay right here. You're more real than those two, anyway. So tell me, Elina Sinclair, why don't you have a date to this shindig?"

She rolled her eyes. "See earlier comment about not being into guys right now."

"Let me guess, career girl. Super focused. About to take the world by storm."

Elina laughed. This was fun. *He* was fun. It felt good to flirt, and laugh. *It can't go any further than this.* But it never hurt the self-esteem to have a good-looking guy hit on her. "It's like you've been following me."

"No, I'm not *that* much of a creeper. I just pay attention. So come on, tell me, what do you do?"

People always got the wrong impression when she talked about her job, so she kept it as simple as possible when anyone asked. "I work in PR." Then she flipped the conversation on him so she wouldn't have to talk about herself. "And what about you? Let me guess, fashion model?"

He laughed. "No, but that's a new one. Usually the girls who take a stab say billionaire."

"Wait." She put her hand on his arm. "So you're telling me you're not one? Ah, that means that we can't talk. I don't always drink champagne, but when I do, I only drink with the disgustingly wealthy."

He laughed, and the low timbre made her insides melt. "You know what, I'll say that persistence is key. I may not be a billionaire but I could be worth your time."

"Okay, if that's not your job—though I always wondered how that can be a job anyway—what is it?"

"Well, soon enough I'm hoping to add filmmaker to my list of talents."

She lifted her brows. "For real? That's amazing. What kind of movies do you want to make?"

"The story of my grandmother. She was a Hollywood executive back in the fifties. The *first* female executive. I've already got my dream cast picked out. All I'm looking for right now is funding."

It was easy to talk to him. He told her about his movie and what inspired his grandmother. And that particular time in Hollywood history. Despite her carefully constructed walls, she told him about herself. About some of her wackiest clients, her friendship with Reece. Even her mother.

Conversation flowed easily. When she relaxed and wasn't so focused on his pretty face, she could talk. It turned out they even liked the same indie hip-hop group. "I'm actually headed to see CJ Fusion in the city next month," he said.

"No way. Reece and I are going to the same concert."

"See, now you have to dance with me. I've proven my cool points." He reached out his hand, and Elina stared down at it for moment. If she took it, she knew she wouldn't want to stop. Being in his arms was too tempting.

Could she throw caution to the wind? She was stuck on a boat, though. So nowhere to go. She might as well have some fun. Sliding her hand into his, she relished the warm buzz it sent through her body. "Okay, lead the way. I warn you, though, I don't normally dance in stilettos, so join me at your own risk."

Gabe liked her. It was just that simple. As she danced and twirled in his arms and gyrated her booty to the latest Top 40 songs, he felt happy, and he was glad to see her smiling instead of that frowning concern. She made him feel lighter.

Eventually, he took her hand and led her off the dance floor, dragging her to the other end of the yacht and down the stairs.

"Hey, isn't this corded off?"

"You hardly seem like a girl who is bothered by the rules."

Elina laughed. "Okay, not usually, but this is someone's yacht. I like you and all, but I'm not willing to do time for you. Orange is not my color."

"Relax, would you? I can usually talk my way out of anything. And I sort of know the owner." Never mind that he *was* the owner. Part owner, anyway. "I want to show you something."

"Oh, I can take a guess at what you want to show me."

If she had been any other girl, he wouldn't be so careful with her. Not to mention, Adam had warned him off. Normally, he'd be leading her back into the bedroom. But instead of heading straight to the sleeping quarters, he veered left and took her into his favorite room.

When he turned on the light, Elina gasped. "Oh my God, this is beautiful."

This room was used specifically for parties. It had a small karaoke stage and comfortable lounge seating. But the most astonishing feature of the room was the see-through glass floor. When the lights in the room were activated, it triggered the lights at the bottom of the yacht, illuminating everything that was beneath them in the ocean.

Already, several curious fish had swum up to take a peek. "You like it?"

"It's awesome." She inclined her head toward the microphone. "What's that for?"

"What do you think it's for? You and Reece were talking yesterday about your mad karaoke skills. I want to see for myself."

She shook her head. "I have not had enough alcohol for that. How did you know this was here, anyway?"

"I have friends." He laughed.

"I guess you do. Okay, then. Since you're so eager for the mic to get some use, how about *you* sing *me* something"

He wasn't sure why he flushed. He was so damn aware of her in the confined space. "Okay, I can sing you a song, but you have to take a seat and be a good audience. Tips are always accepted, in some cases exuberant applause will do just fine, but I prefer panties."

She folded her arms. "You'll have to work harder for my panties. Go on. Get on with it. Let's see these skills of yours."

He booted up the laptop, then pulled up the right track. "Okay, okay. Try not to be a groupie now."

Elina rolled her eyes. "Just sing for your supper, will you?"

"Fine." Then the music started and he closed his eyes. He'd always loved this song. He sang the first line of the song, giving it his all.

Elina squealed with laughter and clapped excitedly. "Oh damn, you're taking on Shai?"

"Would you let a man finish a song?" He continued, dropping the last note to another octave.

Elina rose from her seat laughing and walked toward him. He finished the song and before he knew it, she was up there with him singing. He lost track of how long they sang duets and giant hits from popular bands. Apparently, she was a Journey fan.

Without thinking, he brushed a strand of hair off her face and tucked it behind her ear. He told himself he didn't plan it this way. But it didn't matter if he'd planned it or not. The moment she parted her lips, he knew he was a goner.

Chapter 4

Gabe brushed his lips over hers lightly, testing the waters. Elina sighed into his embrace, and he moaned. His nerve endings were going sizzle and pop. Sliding his fingers into her soft curls, he deepened the kiss. She tasted so sweet. Her lip gloss maybe? Fruity and light. Whatever it was, he liked it.

Gabe slid his tongue between her sinfully soft lips, and she met it with hers. One hand smoothing over her waist, he deepened their kiss. Taking long drugging pulls at her lips and eliciting a moan out of her.

So damn perfect. He felt like someone had hooked his body up to a defibrillator, the kiss was so charged. Their only points of contact were her hands on his waist, his hand in her hair and on her hip, and their lips. But it was enough to send his heart into a gallop and for the blood to rush in his ears.

The kiss shook him. He'd kissed a lot of women. Certainly more than his fair share. But with Elina, his body hummed and his synapses shorted. Tugging her closer, he licked into her mouth. Elina moaned and slid her arms up to wind around his neck.

This was more than *want*. This was more than *lust*. With one kiss, he knew he wanted her as his. How was she doing this to him? Her hands slipped into his hair and gave an impatient tug. She might not be in a guy phase right now, but maybe he could change her mind. Because right now, Elina Sinclair was rocking his soul.

Gabe glided his fingers over the small of her back in the barest hint of a caress and he was shaking. *Damn it.* He pulled back and met her dark gaze. "What are you doing to me, Elina?"

In her eyes he saw desire, uncertainty, trepidation. But he also saw her decision clearly when her beautiful smile spread over her lips. "Are you going to help me with this dress? I had a hell of a time getting the zipper up earlier."

He blinked. What had she said? He was having a hard time concentrating on anything other than how she tasted and how he wanted more. Somehow he could think more clearly when he was kissing her, or maybe that was instinct. She'd said something about her zipper. *Right.* He could do that.

She pressed her body into his as he tugged the zip down. In the silence of the party room, the *zik, zik, zik* sound echoed off the walls with her groans. The dress fell away and over her hips, the fabric fluttering to the ground. Gabe released her and stepped back, and his breath caught. She wore a demi-cup bra and thong in red lace that matched the color of the dress. The material barely covered her nipples, but it did a stand-up job at trying.

He muttered a low curse and tried to swallow around the sawdust in his mouth. "You're so beautiful."

He watched in delight as the pink flush crept up under that pretty caramel skin. Her gaze never wavered from his. She might have been a little shy, but she was confident enough to know what she wanted. She reached back behind her and unclasped her bra, tugging the useless scraps from her breasts and her arms. "See something you want?"

"Hell yes." He nodded, then grunted, as he pulled her close to his chest. He kissed her again, this time taking the kiss even deeper, licking into her mouth, dragging a response from her. All the while he could feel the stiff peaks of her nipples against his chest.

The low moan that came from her throat sounded like a purr, rolling over him like a caress. Gabe picked her up easily and snatched her dress off the floor before carrying her out of the room and down the hall to the bedroom.

When he deposited her on the large bed, he stripped himself of his tux clumsily, letting the pieces fall where they may. Before he kicked out of the tuxedo pants, he grabbed a condom from his wallet and tucked it in the back of his boxer briefs. "You know, there's one thing I've been wondering all night," he whispered against her skin as he crawled up her body.

She smiled at him and arched her back. "What's that?"

Gabe nuzzled her neck with his nose. "How you taste right here." He nipped at the spot behind her ear, but then soothed the injury with a lap of his tongue. "Mmm. Just what I thought. Sweet and spicy."

Elina hooked one of her legs around his back and rocked her hips. Her hot, slick center slid over the cotton-clad length of him and his eyes crossed. *Damn.* He fought for control, fought to stay steady. He didn't want to go too fast. To ruin this.

"Gabe," she moaned. Her breathing harsh and labored

and her back bowed beneath him. He ran his nose along her skin to the hollow of her throat.

"I've been dying to kiss you here, too." He blew a breath over her heated flesh down to one raised breast. Sliding his hands up her torso, he took his time, running his fingers over her ribs and her soft skin. When he palmed her, she moaned, arching into the caress.

Her hips lifted again and again, starting them on a rhythm that wouldn't stop. Placing kisses all along her chest and down her sternum, Gabe teased her nipple with his thumb, tested the weight of her breast, making the both of them crazy. Every time his mouth went near the peaked tip, she writhed beneath him.

He teased the mocha-colored tip with his breath, deliberately making the both of them crazy. He ached to take her into his mouth, to taste her. And by the way she arched her body, she wanted him to. Every time he veered his kiss to the underside of her breast, or down toward a rib, she growled in frustration.

When he finally took the stiff peak in his mouth, she drew in a shuddering breath, and he growled his satisfaction as his hand busied himself with her other breast. Sucking, licking and teasing with his tongue and his teeth he took her to the edge and back again.

Finally, she dug her hands into his hair and held him steady at her breast while she rocked her hips into him. As he sucked, he slid his other hand down, over her taut flat belly, under the flimsy elastic of her thong. Elina's hands clutched at the pillows and her hips bucked into his questing finger.

Oh so gently, Gabe grazed her nipple with his teeth as his finger found her wet and inviting. Slowly, he dipped inside her sex, testing her, seeing how ready she was—

how much she wanted him. He was in no hurry and could do this all night.

This girl was different. This girl was magic. All he wanted to do was see her come alive under his hands.

He released her breast and she whimpered, trying to bring him back. But instead, he kissed his way back up her body. Taking her lips again, he timed his finger with the deep strokes of his tongue.

Against his thigh, his erection throbbed and begged for relief, but this was about her—about seeing her fly. He could wait. Gritting his teeth against the need, he dragged his lips from hers, trailing them along her jawline to her neck, and she shivered.

Her hands traced up his back, her nails digging into his bunched and flexed muscles. "Gabe, please, hurry, I need—" Before she could finish, her slick, slippery flesh quivered around his fingers.

He pulled back to watch her wide-eyed, blissed-out expression. Seeing her lashes flutter closed and her mouth parted on a silent scream of ecstasy, he demanded, "Look at me, Elina. I want you to look at me while you come."

She opened her eyes and met his gaze with a shocked expression as her body tightened around his exploring fingers again. His thumb ghosted over her pleasure button, and his name was a moan on her lips as she came again.

Gabe gentled his strokes, but he didn't stop. He wasn't done with her yet. He wanted her boneless by the time they were done. Then he wanted to start all over again. With each gentle glide, he nuzzled at her neck, sipped at her lips, nipped at the flesh of her collarbone. "How are you feeling, beautiful?"

She giggled and bit her bottom lip. "Warm, and sleepy, and for the first time in a long time, really, really relaxed."

He flicked his thumb over her clitoris again and Elina's

breath hitched. She swallowed her soft gasp as he added another finger. "You still feeling sleepy?" he whispered against her lips.

She shivered and slid her hands in his hair again. "Not so much anymore. I wonder how that happened."

His lips quirked. "I have no idea."

"Gabe, please, I need you. I just—" Her legs clamped around his hips and she broke apart again in his arms.

He grinned to himself as he gently pulled his fingers from her. "What was that you were saying, beautiful?" He rolled away, quickly shucked his boxers and made quick work of the condom he'd tucked away. When he crawled up over her bed, she reached for him.

"Come here," she whispered.

"You don't have to ask me twice." He kissed her again. Pouring everything he had into it. Using his body to communicate the rush of emotion. When he drew back, her eyes were half lidded again and she stroked his hair back tenderly.

"I need you, Gabe."

A shiver ran through him, and he bit his lip. When he lined his erection up with her sweet center and slid home, they both gasped, the breath rushing out of their lungs.

God, she was tight. So tight. It didn't take long before the need was tingling and spiraling along his spine. She stroked his back and met him thrust for thrust, holding eye contact as they made love. Gabe knew then he'd never been as connected to another human being in his life.

When her legs locked around his hips again, he was lost. She pulsed around him, milking his erection, and he finally let the reins of control go. In one stroke, he followed her into blissful oblivion, knowing he would never be the same.

Chapter 5

Elina stretched languorously. That was the best night's sleep she'd had in weeks. The last month or two she'd needed a light sleeping pill to help her get to bed. But last night… God, she needed more nights' sleep like that. Wait, what time was it? She peeled open an eyelid trying to get a good look at her clock.

It was only then that it hit her that she wasn't at home in her own bed. She was in a foreign bed with soft white cotton sheets and a floppy duvet. The sun streamed in from the window, bringing diffused light. Behind her back was a furnace. A *hard* furnace. Then suddenly, that furnace wrapped an arm around her and pulled her close, kissing the nape of her neck.

Then with sudden clarity, she knew *where* she was. She knew *who* she was with, and she knew *what* she had done. *Holy hell.* She'd slept with the best man. Damn Gabe and that crooked smile of his. What was a girl supposed to do?

Jump him, clearly. Okay. Done that, but now what? She wasn't normally so careless, but he'd been sweet, and fun, and there had been karaoke. It wasn't her fault she'd given in. When in doubt, blame the karaoke. He sang Shai to her, for the love of God.

And unlike the rest of Adam's friends, he wasn't just some bored rich kid spending his parents' money. He had dreams, and he was trying to do something with his life. *That doesn't matter now.* Right now, it was time to get out of Dodge.

Elina slipped out from under his arm and froze when he rolled into her closer, as if in search of her heat. *Would it really hurt to linger in bed for just another hour?* Yes, yes it would. She had broken her own cardinal rule number one. No sleepovers. She hadn't had a long-term boyfriend since college, and she wasn't into sleeping around. But she knew what overnights generally meant. *Attachment.* And she wasn't going to do that.

When Gabe rolled over and snuggled her pillow, she stood up slowly and gathered her clothes off the floor. *Holy walk of shame.* Wait, not walk, *swim.* She was still on the damn boat.

Elina dressed hurriedly and told herself she wasn't going to look back at the sleeping Gabe. *Don't look back. Don't look back. Do. Not. Look. Back.* But of course, she turned and looked back. And unfortunately for her lady parts, he was just as good-looking asleep as he was when he was awake and flashing that grin of his.

At this rate, she'd be just as bad as her mother. As she carried her stilettos up the stairs and out, she saw that they were docked in the marina.

Oh God. Reece must be looking for her. She turned on her phone and sure enough, there were five messages from her friend.

"Hey, Elina, where are you? We're about to toss the bouquet and I want you here."

Next message.

"Hey, babe, you're not sick, are you? Are you holed up in the bathrooms puking your guts out? Call me. Find me. I'm worried."

Next message.

"Hey, slacker, is it a coincidence that you and Gabe are missing together? Or did you really decide to swim to shore and ruin that perfectly good Cavalli dress?"

Next message.

"Okay, I'm worried. Even if you're with Gabe, call me as soon as you get this."

She didn't bother to listen to the last message. She knew how it would go. Instead, she called. Checking her watch, she breathed a sigh of relief. It was only seven thirty. Reece and Adam didn't leave for their honeymoon until ten. She wouldn't be interrupting anything…hopefully.

Reece answered on the first ring, and she was not happy. "Where the hell have you been? I have been worried sick. If you hadn't gone missing with Gabe I would've assumed you were man overboard."

Elina skipped down to the dock, or rather did a half run, half skip since the dress had zero give. "I'm so sorry. I swear to God I will make this up to you. I didn't mean to abandon you at your reception."

"What? You think I'm upset because you abandoned me? Dude, you've done your duty. I was married. I was busy dancing my ass off, eating some cake, throwing a bouquet, which you missed incidentally. I was just really worried. It's not like you to vanish."

She felt terrible. "I am so sorry. I don't even know what happened. First we were dancing, and then there was karaoke and…" She let her voice trail off.

"Honey, I'm just giving you a hard time. Now that I know you're okay, can we talk about exactly where you were?"

Elina laughed as she waved down a taxi. "No, we cannot talk about it. Matter of fact, I never want to talk about it. We'll just pretend the whole thing never happened."

"You know you can't get away with that, right? Gabe Alexander? You sly dog, you. I mean, the man is positively smoking, but I thought you weren't in a guy phase?"

"I know what I said about the guy phase thing. And I wasn't. I mean I'm not." Nope, she was just in the Gabe Alexander phase. *Hell.* No, she was not. "It was a onetime thing. We got carried away and that's that."

"Uh-huh? And just where is the yacht-owning lover boy right now?"

Elina winced. "He owns the freaking yacht? That's just fantastic. I may or may not have sneaked out on him."

Reece laughed out loud. That kind of full belly laugh that only her best friend was capable of. "You know what, I'm sure that this is some kind of karmic payback for something he's done in the past. Don't worry about it."

Elina leaned forward and gave the taxi driver the address for her hotel. "Yeah, but I do feel terrible."

Reece stopped laughing. "Oh my God, was he bad?"

Bad? No. Hell no. The man was made for sex. But it had felt like more than just sex. They'd been so connected. And then she'd run out. Like a freaking coward. Elina scrubbed a hand over her face. "No, he is very well practiced."

"I knew it. He's just one of those guys that looks like he moves well, you know?"

Did she ever know. "Look, Reece, this goes into the vault and we don't talk about it. With any luck I won't see him again for a very long time and I can just forget the whole thing ever happened."

"Why do you want to forget if it was good? Especially if he wants to see you again?"

"Reece, have you forgotten who you're talking to?"

Reece sighed. "You're really going to let him slip out of your fingers?"

"He's not mine, Reece. And I've got a different focus now. Someone like him is just going to distract me."

"I know you. You wouldn't have slept with him if you didn't feel a genuine connection. Are you sure this is the best move?"

No, she wasn't sure. And right about now her body was certain it was the wrong plan. But her brain would eventually wake up and realize she'd done the right thing. She was not her mother. Good sex didn't equal love.

Gabe nestled in closer to Elina's scent. When he reached over to her side of the bed to pull her close, it was cold. He blinked awake rapidly, then called out for her, "Elina, are you here?"

But there was no answer. *Oh hell.* She'd left? He sat up in bed and ran his hands through his hair. After last night, she'd actually run away?

His first instinct was to call Adam and Reece and get her number. Not that he was desperate; he was just making sure she was okay… Okay, yeah, that sounded desperate. *What is wrong with you? It's just a girl.* And he'd slept with plenty of girls.

But he never *made love* to one before. He might've only just met her, but that's what it felt like. At the very least, it was one hell of a connection.

He showered quickly before checking in with the captain. He usually split his time between New York and Los Angeles, but his father liked to keep the yacht in the marina here in the Hamptons.

Quickly checking his watch, he hopped in his BMW i8 and made the short drive to Reece and Adam's hotel. The two of them didn't leave for another hour, and he hoped he might be able to catch Elina. Sneak-outs happened to everyone. He may have run out of dozens of beds, but he'd never been left behind before.

He eventually found Adam drinking coffee by the pool and helped himself to a seat and a croissant. "Hey, where's your new wife?"

Adam grinned. "That has a nice flow, doesn't it?"

"Please, spare me from your sappy, lovey-dovey stuff this morning. I need to find Reece."

Adam frowned. "Why, what's up? What do you need?"

Gabe hesitated, but then spit it out. "I'm looking for Elina's number."

Adams smile spread slowly from cheek to cheek, quickly replaced by a frown. "I knew it! Once I saw you guys dancing, I knew the old Gabe Alexander would make an appearance. I thought I warned you against that."

He didn't have time for this. "You did. And it's not like that. I like her."

Adam pinned him with a narrow-eyed glare. "You've liked plenty of girls."

Okay. But Elina was different. "Yeah, but I actually like *talking* to this one."

Adam sat back, crossed his arms and studied him shrewdly. "Holy shit, did you get bitten by the bug?"

A tingle of awareness hopped up Gabe's spine. "I don't know what you mean by bug. I just thought she was cool. So I'm trying to follow up."

"Uh-huh. Sure you are. Dude, I thought you were working on funding and focused on that. Not chasing tail."

"Adam, she's not tail."

"*I* know that, but do you? You have had this habit of being into a girl, then fizzling."

Gabe clenched his jaw. Maybe Adam had a point. Why was he here, really? Because it sucked to be left. She was great, but he did have stuff to focus on. And at the top of the list wasn't Elina Sinclair.

It was a night he wouldn't soon forget, but he was going to have to let her go. He had to. Everything inside him fought against that instinct, but he couldn't be pulled in two directions. Not now. "She's special." He sat back and slouched. "But you're right, I can't focus on her right now."

For now, he'd just have to chalk it up as one of those things and try to put it in the back of his mind.

Chapter 6

On Monday morning, Gabe paced the foyer of D. Donovan Image Consultants as he tried to shake off the residual effect of Elina Sinclair. He'd managed okay the rest of yesterday in the Hamptons, and even this morning. But as soon as he hit the city and parked, he would have sworn he saw Elina somewhere near Soho, walking uptown. Just what he needed right before he had to beg Delilah Donovan to take him on as a client.

"Hiya," said a pretty redhead. "You must be Gabe. I'm Willow. Come on back. I'll take you to Delilah."

He shook hands with the slim woman, and followed her down the hall toward the bank of offices. "It's nice to meet you. This is a great space."

"Thanks. It took us about a year and a half to get it just right. But we love it."

Willow didn't look like any fixer he'd ever met before. She wore leather pants and plenty of eyeliner, and her tattoos were on full display with her sleeveless top. "How long have you guys been here now?"

"Gosh, it's been almost two years now. We were at Park & Associates before." She shrugged. "But it's better being on our own."

"How big is the team?"

"We're a boutique agency, so just three of us. Delilah and I are partners. We also have a junior associate. I know you're wondering if a small agency can handle your needs, but I promise you, we know what we're doing."

"I'm not worried. I was told that Delilah was the best. And I believe it."

"I'm glad to hear that, Mr. Alexander, because I plan on making you work."

He turned to find Delilah Donovan in the doorway. She was maybe five feet four inches, but it was hard to tell in her stacked boots. The sunlight behind her made her skin look like a mix of cinnamon and honey. She wore her hair in a sleek bun on top of her head, but her clothing was casual leggings and some kind of tunic. Not fussy.

He shook her hand. "Thank you for taking the time to meet with me. I appreciate you fitting me in."

Delilah gave him a warm smile. "Pleased to meet you. I have to admit, you're different than I thought. I thought I'd get the hard partier, but you look good."

He shifted on his feet. "In that case I'm happy to disappoint."

She and Willow took seats across from him. "So, why don't you tell us what you're looking for? Your manager called in a favor and I'm happy to help, but I want to know in your own words what you think you need."

"At this point I'm looking to restart my career, but more on the production development side. I'm not opposed to acting again, but I really want to set myself apart from my father. And to distance myself from that pissed-off kid who was drunk all the time and slept with too many starlets." The years of fifteen to twenty were pretty much a blur.

Delilah nodded. "Why, though? From what I understand you were smart with your money. It could've gone in the opposite direction, given how hard you were going. Why do you want to open yourself back up to that kind of scrutiny?"

It was a good question. "Because I love to create. And I have a story that won't leave me alone. I just need the financial backing to get it made. And given my history, no one's exactly lining up to give me money. I can fund some of it myself, but I know I'll need more money than that."

She nodded. "You're right. You *will* need more money. So why don't you tell us about your script?"

For the next thirty minutes he walked them through his plan, his cast and the story. They were receptive and thought his idea was good. Delilah leaned forward, placing her elbows on her knees, and folded her hands. "Okay, talking to you, I see that you mean this. I rarely sign on entertainment clients anymore. Been burned too many times by people who wanted paparazzi placements as opposed to legitimate media. I think we can work together, but I have a specific set of rules."

"Okay, I can work with rules."

"You need to be above reproach when it comes to women. I suggest steering clear of any potential land mines for a while. No sneaking out to starlets' rooms at night. No going back with some random at a concert or anything like that. Squeaky-clean until you get the funding you need. No perception of impropriety. You had one hell of a rep. We need to make you into a new man. One who is all about the work."

He nodded. "I can do that. Whatever it takes. I don't

want anything to get in my way. Whether you choose to help me or not."

She smiled and sat back. "Now that's the kind of client I'm looking for." There was a buzz from the front of the office that signaled someone was there. And when the door to the conference lounge opened, Gabe knew he was about to break every promise he'd just made.

Delilah smiled. "Hey, Elina. You're just in time to meet our latest client. This is Gabe Alexander, and we'll be working with him for the next several months."

Gabe slid his gaze to Elina and held his breath. Her wide-eyed stare told him everything he needed to know. She'd never intended to see him again.

Chapter 7

How was this her life? Most people never saw their random hookups again. Not Elina. Her hookup was sitting there, in a meeting with her boss. And of course she was supposed to smile and nod at him. Which she barely managed.

As soon as the meeting was over, Elina tried to book it out of the office. "I'm just going to make a quick coffee run. Anyone need anything?"

Willow called out, "I'll take my usual from the coffee cart off Porter."

Delilah called, "The same."

She didn't really expect Gabe to have a coffee order. She also didn't expect that he would come with her. "I'll just go and help carry it all back. Plus, the least I can do is buy you guys coffee."

Shit. She moved faster. It didn't matter that she was trying to avoid him; he caught up to her quickly enough. "You don't have to follow me. Why don't you just go back to the office and I'll bring you whatever you need."

Gabe kept his voice low as she stormed onto the downtown streets. "*You* are what I need right now, or at least, an answer. Did you know you abandoned me?"

"I didn't abandon you. I had to catch the jitney back to the city." Mostly true.

"Are you serious right now?" He glared at her.

Okay, that was a flimsy excuse. But it was all she had at the moment. There was no way she was telling him she ran because she couldn't handle the connection she'd felt. "Look, these things happen."

He sputtered. "These things happen? Not to me they don't."

"What are you doing here?" she spat. "In case you didn't know, when you hook up with someone, they're not supposed to turn up the next day. That's like a rule or something. Or it should be."

"Maybe you should stop having random nights out with random dudes."

"Don't do that."

"Do what?" Exasperated, he threw his hands up.

She stiffened her spine, turning back and marching towards Delilah's favorite coffee cart. "Look, what happened, happened. The best we can do is to pretend it didn't. We're gonna go back and act like we don't know each other, because we don't when you think about it."

He blinked at her. "That's what you seriously want?"

"Maybe you don't know Delilah, but she has a full-disclosure policy and she doesn't mess around with it. From what I just heard in there, you need her. If she finds out that we slept together, she'll drop you, given your reputation."

"What will she do to you?"

Elina didn't want to think about that. "Well, then I can just kiss the career I worked so hard for goodbye. You need your film and I need my job. So we don't know each other."

He pulled her into an alley by the coffee cart. "You can do that? Pretend? That Saturday night never happened?"

She tilted her chin up. "Yeah, and given your rep, I know you can."

His brows snapped down. And then before she knew it, his lips were on hers. Harsh and firm and demanding. His tongue delved into her mouth and demanded she respond. Traitor that her body was, she melted as if today was a continuation of Saturday night and Sunday morning. She knew that when it came to him, she was weak. She wouldn't be able to stop.

Gabe pulled back. "Still want to pretend we don't know each other?"

Elina scowled and pushed his broad shoulders back. "Yes. As far as you and I are concerned, we've never met." Now all she needed was to tell her body that.

Chapter 8

After a week of working with Gabe, Elina was ready to lose her mind. Normally clients didn't post up in the office, but given the urgency to get him in some festivals, he had camped out.

Plus, he had this whole thing about proving his commitment. Willow and Delilah seemed impressed; she, however…was not.

Every time she turned around, he was there. She said his name more times in a day than she said her own. Over the last week, she called all the studio reps in Delilah's contacts to set up meetings with him. She sent out scripts. She got him coffee. She worked with managers to determine cast availability. Next on her list for tomorrow was to call the film festivals to create some buzz around his project. The closest ones coming were Montreal, Toronto and Sundance.

Sundance was so competitive these days it would be

difficult to get into that one, but Montreal and Toronto were good bets.

Long after Delilah and Willow left for the night, she finally snapped her laptop shut only to discover that Gabe was still in the meeting lounge on a call with the West Coast. Damn it, she couldn't leave without him. She had to close up. She ended up lurking around for another thirty minutes before he was done.

He looked up with an apologetic smile. "Hey, sorry about that. Delilah said I should go ahead and finish the calls here."

She bit her tongue. "No, it's fine. Let's go and I'll lock up."

They'd managed to pretend they didn't know each other well enough. She didn't think Willow or Delilah had any suspicions. But as the firm's investigator, Willow had her ways of finding things out, so they needed to be extra careful around her.

They walked out of the building, and Gabe shoved his hands in his jeans and rocked onto his heels while she secured the front door. "So, how do you think we did this week?"

She sighed. "I think it's fine. Willow is tricky, though. We'll just have to keep from being too familiar."

Never mind that instinctual need to reach out and brush his hair or straighten his tie. Which was ridiculous, because she didn't know him like that. *Let's face it, you like touching him.* Yeah, that was the problem. A week ago, she'd been caressing him all over. *That won't help you. Don't think about that.*

Gabe nodded. "Are you getting a cab or taking the subway?"

"Oh, don't worry. I live about ten blocks that way, in the Village. I'll be fine. It's pretty safe."

He frowned. "You realize you just used the word *safe* in reference to New York City?"

"Yes, because it is. I make this walk all the time. The trans-hookers three blocks over know me by name."

He sputtered a laugh. "I'm not sure that's a good thing."

"Okay, maybe not, but it's fine. You don't have to walk me home or anything. You can check your chivalry card off for the night."

"Well, it looks like my card will have to remain unchecked for a bit longer as I also live in the Village, on Tenth."

Seriously? Of course he would live four blocks away from her. Though his place was no doubt more posh than hers. Her apartment was actually Willow's old apartment. Thanks to the rent-control, she could actually afford it. "I guess you're going my way, then."

He chuckled. "Don't look so happy about it."

This was harder than she thought. "Look, it's not that I'm unhappy, I just didn't expect to see you again, so it's been a long week. And having to pretend doesn't make it any easier."

"You think it's easy for me to go along with this charade? When all I keep thinking about is how you taste?"

She stopped and glared at him. "You know you can't say that to me right?"

"Yes, Elina, I know." He rolled his eyes. They walked in silence for a block before he asked, "Can I ask you a question, though?"

"Why do I get the feeling I'm going to regret this question?"

"It's a simple question."

"Okay, shoot."

"Why did you leave that morning?"

Of course he would ask her that. She chewed on her

bottom lip as she figured out her answer. "The truth?" It was easier to talk to him when they were walking and she didn't have to look directly into his hypnotic eyes.

"Always."

"I really don't do relationships, or messy situations. And I liked you. Probably more than I should have. But our best friends just got married. Sleeping with you was the messiest decision I've ever made. And I figured a clean break was ideal."

Gabe turned to her and gave her his lopsided smile. Her heart flipped over. *Stupid heart.* "I scared the shit out of you?"

Despite herself, she laughed. "Yeah, something like that. We had fun. *A lot* of fun. It's just way too complicated." Elina licked her lips nervously, "So, since we're being honest?"

Gabe rolled his eyes as he laughed. "Go on, ask me anything you want."

"You mean besides where you learned that thing with your tongue?"

His bark of laughter bounced off of the buildings around them. "Yeah, you probably don't want to know the answer to that!"

"No, probably not. But I do want to ask why you were so upset. I mean, now that I know who you are, it's clear you have a certain reputation. And have access to plenty of women. So why were you so focused on me?" She braced herself for the truth. There was a part of her that wanted to be special, but the rational part of her wanted it to be about the game.

He considered his answer, and then he opted for the truth. It was easier that way. "At first, it was a little bit about the chase. I'm not used to being told no. But then, at the wedding, when you looked so sad, I just wanted to make you smile. I didn't plan what happened. That's not my MO or anything. Meet hot chick, take her down to the bedrooms in the yacht. I just thought we'd have fun. I felt connected to you. And then you were gone."

She nodded. "Why didn't you tell me it was your yacht?"

"Would you have lumped me in with the rest of Adam's bratty, rich-kid friends?"

She scrunched her nose. "Maybe. But not once we started talking."

"I guess you live and learn." For the next several blocks they talked about work and where they went to school.

He asked her something else he'd been dying to know. "Okay, another question for you. Why are you so anti-anything? From the sounds of it you don't even want a relationship, or to date."

She adjusted her laptop bag on her shoulder, and he just reached over and took it from her. "If you knew my mother, you would understand."

"Go on, tell me."

Elina slid him a glance. "Don't say I didn't warn you." She shook her head. "My mother is warm and vivacious and fun. She's also a total addict."

Wow. Not what he'd been expecting. "I'm sorry, Elina, that must've been rough."

She shook her head. "It's not what you think. She's addicted to love. She gets high off a new relationship. The dramatics of dating. And the dramatics of divorce. She's been married seven times. *Three* of those to my father."

Some of this he knew from Adam. But it was still unbelievable to hear. "Holy shit. Are you serious?"

"Yeah. I wish I was kidding. She has six ex-husbands."

"Seriously?"

"Yeah. So growing up, she would have a guy, then get

bored, and instead of working it out, she would just divorce him."

"That seems a little drastic."

"You don't know the half of it. She will invent bogus reasons for why she can no longer be with said husband. The very same reasons, mind you, that were red flags to begin with. It's like she suddenly wakes up from the haze and realizes that she's overdosed. But then, instead of acting like an adult and sticking it out or getting therapy, she ditches and runs. Only to repeat the same experience six months later. I really thought that last time with my father, it would stick. But it didn't. He died a year later. She's never been the same. I think in the long run, she thought they'd end up together."

"Wow, that must have been insane growing up."

"So weddings for me aren't exactly a fairy-tale endeavor. I've seen too many of them. Been forced into too many bridesmaids dresses, walked my mother down the aisle too many times. I've watched her pour sand, light candles, break glass. All of it."

"All right, then. I get it. No weddings. You must really love Reece to be part of hers."

At the mention of Reece's name, Elina's shoulders relaxed and she beamed. "She's seen me through many a divorce. So for her, I would do just about anything."

"That also explains your somewhat haunted look at the ceremony."

She shrugged. "I love Adam. I think they're great together. I just know how easily marriages can fall apart. And with that piece of paper, things just get messier and uglier. They can be together and not get married."

"You mean together forever."

"Yeah, it's kind of romantic. You know, not needing to make it official. No piece of paper will hold anyone there."

He chuckled. "For someone who says that's romantic, you also seem to be anti-relationship."

"I'm not a giant fan," she mumbled. "Last guy I dated long-term was back in college. I mostly don't want to turn into her."

Well, damn, that made a lot more sense. "And then you get a guy like me who won't leave you alone."

She laughed. "It's not exactly like I want you to leave me alone, but now it's complicated, *very* complicated. And I'm not very good at all the relationship stuff anyway."

"You're telling me that you haven't had a boyfriend since college. And nobody's giving it a shot? I find that hard to believe."

"I date. I just don't date *often*. And with my job it's easier to focus on that. Everything with Mom was always about 'Does he like me?' 'Is he into me?' 'How can I make him *more* into me?' And I don't want my life to be about that. There has to be something else out there."

"Do you want your life to be all about work?"

She drew up her shoulders. "No, not exactly."

He could tell he was making her antsy. "Well, inquiring minds want to know. I might know a million ways to make your body hum. And I also know your go-to karaoke songs, but I'm curious about *you*."

"You know what they say about curiosity and the cat, right?"

Gabe grinned. "That he had a hell of a time using his nine lives?"

She laughed. "Fine, I'm not *opposed* to a relationship. It would be nice to come home and talk to somebody. But I also don't want that to define me. I don't want to be so crazy trying to hold on to a feeling that I lose myself."

He could understand that. All his life, he watched people chase fame. And it had never made any of them happy.

Even if they did manage an elusive grasp. "So as far as you're concerned, there's no danger in losing yourself if you never put yourself out there."

"It's easier that way."

He had to laugh at that. "Oh, you call this easier?"

She chuckled, too, and bumped his shoulder with hers. "You know what I mean. Maybe this exact situation isn't easier. But generally. Last weekend was an anomaly for me."

Their gazes met for a prolonged moment, and his body's response was immediate. He was so desperate to touch her. He'd even take holding her hand at the moment. But he didn't. "Me, too, actually. I was a mess before, but I've cleaned up my act. Since then, you're the first girl I've been with in a while. This image that everyone has of me is outdated and based on a series of half-truths. I'm not some crazy womanizer. I watched my dad run around with all these women, and he was never happy. I don't want that." He still remembered that day his grandmother sat him down after she caught him sneaking some girl out of her house. She'd asked him if he liked any of these women. Really liked them. Did he see himself in any of them? If they made him feel happy. Or if they were just an attempt to fill a hole. He'd never really thought about it. Women were always available. But no, so many of them he hadn't liked. At least not enough to see them in the morning. He'd pulled back after that.

"So you mean you're not bedding supermodels?"

Gabe grinned. "There might have been a supermodel or two in my dating past, but right now, I'm focused on building a career I can be proud of. Where I stand on my own two feet. That's what I'm excited about. Not the latest party. Not the next model du jour. Instead, something real."

"So you don't take all women into your secret karaoke room?"

He laughed. "Nope. You're the only woman I've taken down there. I rarely ever use it. You were fun, and I liked you."

She squirmed. "And now everything is mad complicated."

"You can say that again," he muttered.

"So how come you don't want to go back to acting? I viewed your film reel. You were really good."

It had been a long time since anyone referred to him as a good actor. It had been a long time since anyone had referred to him as a good anything. "Thank you. I used to love it. But all the comparisons to Dad, it didn't make me happy. Hell, it never did. I eventually did things I thought would make me happier."

They made a left at Bleecker Street Pizza. "How did that work out for you?"

"These days there's this handy thing called the internet. If you look back about three years and Google my name, you can see for yourself how happy it made me."

"So now you're trying something different?" She slid her gaze over him, and the simple glance was enough to make his muscles bunch and his skin prickle with heat. "It looks good on you."

"So what you're saying is, you think I'm hot."

She bumped him again as she laughed. *Yes, more contact.* It was official, he needed help. "I said no such thing."

"Really? Because that's what I heard in my head. *Gabe is totally hot.*" He tapped his temple. "The Elina that lives in my head, that's what she says."

"Let me guess, in your head she's wearing a lot less clothing?"

He put a hand over his heart. "You wound me. In my head, she's wearing red."

Her skin flushed light pink under that pretty brown skin. She stopped walking in front of a dark wrought-iron gate. "This is me."

Beyond the gate sat a lush courtyard. He could see the inner doorway from where they stood.

He'd been in this position a million times, facing a beautiful woman, determining if she wanted him to kiss her or not. But this wasn't a date, was it? "Well, Elina, it was fun getting to know you."

Her smile was shy as she tucked her hair behind her ear. "Yeah, it was. And I owe you an apology for the first day. And for Sunday morning. I shouldn't have left like that." She paused. "I was being a coward. And that wasn't fair."

He nodded. "It's okay. I get it. I've snuck out of more beds than I should probably admit to. And I was as dumbstruck as you were. I'd just promised Delilah I wouldn't mess with women and be the picture of propriety. Then you walked in. So yeah."

She looked down at her feet. "Well, good night."

He was so desperate to kiss her. Just one taste was all he needed. Though who was he kidding? One taste and he'd be carrying her upstairs, and he wouldn't let her out for days. So for once, Gabe did the smart thing. He leaned into her, but instead of kissing her sweet, soft lips, he kissed her on the cheek, then forced himself to pull back. "Good night, Elina. I'll see you Monday."

Chapter 9

Elina rolled over in her bed. This was Gabe's fault. She hadn't slept a wink all night, tossing and turning, thinking about his infectious crooked smile and those ridiculously amazing eyes of his. It wasn't fair. Why couldn't she just quash that fluttery feeling she got every time she was around him?

This last week had been torture. Seeing him every other day and sometimes working late with him had her ready to climb the walls. It was one thing to have him around. It was a whole other thing to catch him watching her. Her skin would prickle with awareness when she looked up to meet his gaze. It was too easy to get trapped in his hypnotic eyes.

And then, predictably, she'd lose her train of thought and look like a moron in front of the boss she was trying to impress. More than once, Willow asked if she was okay.

Elina dragged a pillow over her eyes. If she could just

get him out of her head and forget about every touch, every lingering caress, every kiss, the way he watched her as they made love.

More than once this week, she had some flash memory of that night. All it would take was a shy smirk, a look, his laugh; basically, all he had to do was stand there and she was assaulted with memories of that night.

Her phone rang on her nightstand and she dragged her pillow off to see who was calling. She didn't know why she bothered; the only person who would call this early was her mother. "Hi, Mama."

"Oh, there you are, baby. I called you yesterday. Didn't you get my messages?"

Elina sighed. It was far too early in the morning for this conversation. "I was working, Mom, what's up?"

"Honestly, darling, it sounds like you're still in bed."

"Mom, it's six thirty in the morning. You're in Toronto, it's the same time for you there. Six thirty is too early to call someone."

"Oh, sweetheart, I've been awake for ages. Early morning really is the best time for yoga. I've got this new yogi. He's very cute so it helps motivate me to get out of bed."

Oh my God. Dealing with her mother before coffee seemed like cruel and unusual punishment. "Are you just calling to chat, Mom? Because if you are, then let me call you back when I'm more awake."

"What's the matter with you, Elina? You're usually more sprightly in the morning."

Elina forced herself to sit up. It might be too early in the morning to talk to her mother, but for some reason she wasn't as irritated as she normally was. *Maybe because you understand her a little now.* "I didn't sleep that well."

"It's that job, sweetheart. I'm telling you. You're too young to spend all your days working."

Elina couldn't help but sputter a laugh. "Mom, now is the time to work my butt off so I can relax later. Now is the time I have energy. Besides, I'm not stressed out about my job. I love my job. And my boss is going give me my own client soon. I'm just tired."

Her mother gasped. "The only thing that will keep a woman up like that is a man. Elina Sinclair, do you have a boyfriend? Will wonders never cease. Who is he? Tell me everything!"

Oh no. Elina flashed back to when she got her first boyfriend in high school. All of a sudden, her mother wanted to chat with her about who the cutest boys in school were. There was no way she was discussing her sex life with her mother. It didn't matter how cool her mother thought she was. "I don't have a boyfriend, Mom."

"Well, that just astounds me, because there is no reason a pretty girl like you shouldn't have a boyfriend."

"I don't want one, Mom. I'm good on my own."

"Yes, but sweetheart, a woman has needs."

Elina felt a wave of nausea wash over her. "We are not talking about this. I have to go." She shuddered.

"Yes, yes, darling, of course you don't want to discuss your love life with me, but if you change your mind I'm a great resource."

"Ewww. Mom!"

"Fine, but I am calling for a reason."

Elina's relaxed goodwill was rapidly evaporating. "Yeah, what is it?"

"I wanted to let you know that I'm getting married again. To Luke. My yogi. We're going to do a very simple, nonmaterialistic, nondenominational ceremony. But obviously I need my best maid of honor there."

Too numb to speak, all Elina could do was force her lungs to work. *Married. Again.* After that last time with her father, her mother had insisted she was never getting married again. Elina should have known that was too good to be true.

After several attempts, she finally found her voice. "So I should ignore all that stuff you said after you divorced Daddy. That I should stop you if you said you wanted to get married again?"

"Oh, sweetheart. You know how I get. At those moments, all I can see is the bad. So what do you say? We still have some time, but you'll make yourself available to be my maid of honor?"

And because she knew she had no choice, Elina whispered, "Sure, Mom. I'll be your maid of honor." She'd been through this cycle before. Hopefully, her mother would gain some sense before the actual wedding date. Elina could only hope.

Chapter 10

On Wednesday, Gabe passed Elina the popcorn before hitting Playback on the video. "So I had my two favorite actors, both unknown, just sit down and do a table read of the first few scenes so I could get a feel for how it flows."

Elina took a handful of popcorn and pushed the bowl back, careful not to touch him. "These actors are really good. Where did you find them?"

He stifled the disappointment. "They're actually NYU students. I saw them at a showcase about a year ago. I have worked with one of the guys' older brother before and he turned me on to his brother's work."

"Seriously, Gabe, these guys are future breakout stars."

"Thanks. I'm lucky they want to work with me."

"That says a lot about the script."

He tried not to let the compliment go to his head. But he loved that Elina was excited about his work, that she believed in him.

It had been a battle for him not to call her over the weekend. Just to talk or hang out, or maybe get naked. No. No getting naked. As much as he wanted her, Delilah was already making strides with his reputation and he didn't want to risk making her angry. She'd already managed to get him a sit-down with several studio executives. The same studios, when his manager called, they'd given them the run around. Now he was at the table. And it was far better to be there than be on the phone begging someone for a meeting.

But, even as Elina avoided touching him or looking directly at him, he could tell something was wrong. They'd made progress on Friday night. They were sort of friends now, right?

"You want to tell me what's bugging you? You've been off all day. When I saw you Monday you were quiet, something I'm learning is unusual for you. Do you need to talk to Reece?" Maybe this was some kind of best-friend emergency or something.

Elina shook her head. "Nah, this'll keep."

She shut down the DVD player and straightened her files. "Remember, we've booked you for the Montreal and Toronto film festivals. Delilah turned over every contact she had and called in a lot of favors. You'll sit on a panel in Montreal, specifically discussing the relationship between actor and director and how you plan to put your spin on it with your project. You also have several interviews about your project while you're there. Toronto is a month after that and we'll do the same thing. Build the buzz."

"Yeah, okay. Sounds great. But I'm not worried about that right now. Right now I'm worried about you. What's wrong?"

Elina's gaze flickered to the door. Delilah had gone home for the night, but Willow was in the apartment next door to the office. "I don't want to talk about it here, okay? I just want to go home, take off my shoes and pass out."

"Do you want to grab food or something? Maybe some takeout?" Damn, he sounded desperate. He wanted to spend time with her, so he'd do what it took. "Good thing we have the whole walk back to your place to decide." Sooner or later she was going to talk to him. He might as well help her make it sooner.

Elina knew she was on edge. Ever since her mother's call Saturday, she hadn't been able to focus or think. That was probably also because her mother had called no less than twenty times since to discuss wedding plans.

The last thing she needed was the constant reminder that she had her mother's genes, that she could manifest feelings for just about anyone. Even some guy she met for one hot night in the Hamptons. To be fair, Gabe wasn't just *any* guy. He wasn't some random. He was really sweet, and right now, doing his best to be her friend.

He followed her out of the building and waited while she locked up. "You might as well say yes. I'm not going to let you walk all the way home by yourself." He shrugged. "*And* you need to eat."

She started down the street at a fast clip, her platform heels making a *clack* and *clomp* sound as her stride ate pavement. "Gabe, thank you for being so nice to me. But I'm in a crappy mood and to be honest I don't really have time for dinner or a drink. My mother wants me to deal with the flower arrangements. And to pick her caterer, vegan of course, and she wants my opinion on all her dresses, and she wants it done this week. If I don't do it this week, she'll just keep calling until I do. So I just want to go home and—"

He pulled her under an awning, out of the way of the

pedestrians on the street. "Wait, she's getting married? Again?"

"That's funny, because your reaction mimics my own. But she's my mother, so not much I can do except smile and nod and let her do what she wants. Never mind that she's going to get divorced in a few months and I'll be left to also pick up those pieces."

"Have you considered just telling her no?"

She blinked. "Have I considered—" Elina sputtered. "The last time someone told Gigi Meyers Sinclair James Adams Sinclair Thomas Stoya Sinclair no, she divorced them. This is a pattern of hers. She gets all excited and it's my job to be excited for her. And then she figures it out eventually, that the guy she's gung ho about isn't the right guy. Most of us call that dating. My mother, she calls it auditioning new husbands. Not all of them make it to the altar. I'm hoping this guy is one of those."

"Oh, Elina, I'm sorry. I can't imagine how frustrating this must be for you. How can I help?"

"You can help by not being so damn nice to me. You're like that perfect guy. You're ridiculously gorgeous, and you have that charming lopsided smile and those eyes that can see clear into my soul. Did you know you have flecks of blue and brown and yellow in them? It's very distracting and hard to look away. I try to look away all the time." Time to stop talking.

She threw her head back and covered her face. "And you have to stop looking at me like that." She was losing it. *Keep your mouth shut, Elina.* The tears pricked her eyes and she rapidly blocked them away behind her hands. She was not going to cry in front of him.

Before she knew what was happening, Gabe pulled her into an embrace. He tucked her head under his chin and he held her. It wasn't sexual in any way. It wasn't even all that intimate. It was just one friend holding another. And damn it felt so good. He was warm and solid and smelled amazing. Her body melted into his, and for the first time since Saturday morning, she relaxed.

"It's okay to say you're not fine with this. It's all right to be irritated and pissed off about it. You don't have to keep it together." He loosened his grasp and went to release her but she held on. She didn't want to let go. Not yet. *Just another minute of torture, please.*

This is a bad idea. For so many reasons. She looked up at him and focused on his lips. Perfectly sculpted, they were already tipping into her favorite smile. *He's an actor. He probably uses that smile all the time.* It didn't matter to her, because right now she felt like the only woman in the world.

"You keep looking at me like that, Elina, and I'm going to do something we'll both regret. Well, more you than me, but still."

She blinked away the sting of rejection and pulled herself out of his hold. He was right. She was stepping over a line she had drawn herself. She shuffled her feet and ducked her head. "Yeah, you're right. I think I just want to order takeout and veg. Thank you for the hug and the chat and whatnot, but my place is only three blocks from here and maybe it's time to call it a night."

"Elina, don't shut down on me. Not when we're making progress. You're running, just like you did on the yacht."

A flash of anger coursed through her. "You don't even know me. You think a couple of kisses and a hug and we're be—"

He cut her off with a kiss. It had quickly become her favorite argument-ender. She moaned into his mouth as she tried to hold on. His lips were firm, demanding. When he dug his hands into the hair at the nape of her neck, heat pooled in her core.

He held her still as he devoured her mouth, never losing contact, barely letting her come up for air. His tongue delved into her mouth and his teeth grazed her bottom lip every time he pulled back.

With his other hand, he held her body tight against his, sliding it just over her ass and cupping her against him.

And then just like that, he released her and staggered back. As he dragged in deep breaths, he glared at her. "You can't *not* know how much I want you." Gabe ran both hands through his hair and shoved his hands in his pockets and took another deliberate step away from her. "But you've made it clear that's not what you want from me, so I'm trying to be respectful and be your friend. But so you know, I think about that night in the Hamptons every night. I can practically feel you responding to me every night. I want you so bad. Your body sliding over mine. Wet and ready. It's driving me insane." He cleared his throat. "But you don't need the guy who wants you naked. You need the guy who wants to make you smile. And I'm going to be *that* guy. No matter how much I'd rather be the *other* guy."

Damn it, now she really was going to cry. "Do you have to be so damn perfect?"

His lips quirked. "If you like, tomorrow, I'll try to be a little less perfect. But right now, I'm going to walk you home. Then we're going to order takeout. Maybe even rent a movie, and you can forget all about wedding nightmares for a night."

She could certainly use a night off from her mother's madness. "Okay, that sounds like a deal." Then she added quietly, "Thank you. To both those guys."

Chapter 11

Elina couldn't focus on anything. Not with Gabe sitting so close. They'd picked one of his favorite movies tonight, *Inside Man*. And there was enough garlic on their pizza to make sure that neither one of them wanted to kiss the other. But that didn't stop her from feeling every single movement he made.

Every breath, every laugh, every bunch of his muscles. She was *that* aware of him. She even considered excusing herself to give herself a break in the bathroom. But she wanted to be close to him.

Man, you really are an addict. Just like her. Elina licked her lips, and she could still taste him. Shifting in her seat and trying to get more comfortable, she ignored the pulsing between her thighs.

Gabe slid his gaze over her. He opened his mouth, but then snapped it shut.

"What? What were you going to say?"

"It's nothing. And it's not helpful."

"You realize that you're driving me crazy, right?" She wanted to smack the smug expression off his face.

"Yeah, I know." He shrugged, then laughed. "Come on. Lean back, just relax. It's fine. We can be friends. We can ignore the attraction. We're two grown-ups."

Right about now, Elina felt like a hormonal teenager. But she took his advice. Carefully eyeing him, she settled into the crook of his arm and leaned back against him. His scent wrapped around her and all she wanted to do was snuggle in deep.

It took her thirty minutes, but she finally relaxed. She liked the feeling of being held. It was nice. Better than nice. Being in his arms could be addictive.

As they watched the movie, his fingers carelessly toyed with the ends of her hair, and more than once she had to stifle a moan. He wasn't doing anything erotic per se, but his fingers in her hair felt incredible.

Near the end of the film, though, he transitioned to smoothing it just off her cheek, and she turned to face him.

Gabe met her gaze. His heart thundered against hers and he couldn't swallow. If they did this, they couldn't go back. He knew that, and so did she. That didn't stop him from wanting. With each shallow breath she drew, her breasts shifted up and down and dragged his attention away from her beautiful face. "Elina. I want you." He shook his head, trying to shake off the wave of lust. "But I want to give you what you asked for. Do you want to do this? Because if you do, that changes things."

Her tongue peeked out to moisten her lips, and her gaze never left his. "All I know is I care about you. Is that enough for now?"

His heart pinched. That wasn't what he needed to hear.

He needed to hear that she wanted him for more than just tonight. More than just a blistering night between the sheets. But the truth was he wanted her any way he could have her.

He settled her away from him and stood up, before extending a hand out to her. For what seemed like a lifetime, she stared at it, as if weighing her decision. As if mulling over the consequences of each action. But then she stood, sliding her hand into his.

He exhaled a long breath of relief. "Where's the bedroom?"

Her lips trembled when she spoke. "Down the hall to the left."

The last time they'd been together, it was so frenzied. *This* was deliberate action. He tugged her down the darkened hall and pulled her through the nearest door. Thankfully, she had a dimmer so when the lights turned on, a soft glow washed over everything.

Her room looked like her. Classic and chic, but unfussy. And organized. He pulled her close and slid his fingers into her hair. He kissed her softly, and still felt like he'd been hooked up to a live wire. But he was determined to take it slow and not rush through everything like the last time.

That had been the plan, anyway. But then she touched her tongue to his, and he lost his grip on control. The blood from his thinking brain rushed to his dick, and suddenly he was wondering why he was being so careful with her. *Because you love her.*

He pulled back from the kiss and gulped in a deep breath. *Hell.* What? He couldn't focus with her standing so close, pressing her body into him. He kissed her again. This time deepening it, letting his tongue explore, making her moan. This he knew how to do. He understood seduction. He understood lust. He knew dozens of ways to make her come. The thing he didn't know anything about was love.

But maybe for once he could try it. With this girl. It might be worth putting himself out there. Trying. Because what he did know was he'd never felt like this before. Gabe poured everything he had into the kiss. She might be afraid to fall for someone, but he could show her that she didn't have any reason to be afraid of him.

Elina trembled under Gabe's hands from the butterfly staccato touches of his fingertips along her spine. She wanted hard and fast and desperate and hungry. But instead, he was giving her soft, sweet, seduction. Tenderness and…love.

The primal, instinctual part of her told her to run. To put as much distance between the two of them as possible. But she didn't. It felt too good being in his arms. He was right. There was no going back after this. They couldn't pretend it hadn't happened. And there was certainly no way he was letting her run from this tomorrow. She wouldn't be able to retreat and put distance between them. He would make her deal with the feelings.

His fingertips massaged her lower back briefly before sliding over her ass and pulling her flush against him. Bringing her aching center into contact with the firm length of his thick erection. And then Elina did something she didn't like to do very often. She surrendered to him, to the kiss. To the possibility.

She moaned into his mouth, and he wasted no time with the T-shirt she'd thrown on once they arrived at her place. Her bra was gone next. His hands skimmed up her torso, taking the time to caress every inch of her skin. Like he was trying to memorize it. "You are so beautiful," he whispered against her lips.

"Gabe, I—"

He kissed her again and cut her off. Elina moaned, looping her arms around his neck.

His skilled hands had her out of her shorts and underwear in seconds. When his fingertips trailed over her sex, he groaned. "You're so wet already. Is that because of me?"

She swallowed around the sawdust in her mouth. "Yes."

A shiver racked his whole body, and he picked her up, gently depositing her on her bed. Making quick, haphazard work of his own clothes, he tossed them aside before joining her.

He knew just how to make her body hum. How she liked her nipples sucked, how much pressure, how little. Shifting his weight to her other nipple, he licked the tip into his mouth as he slipped a finger inside. Elina hissed and dug her hands into his hair, and Gabe muttered a curse against her flesh as he gently penetrated her. Gently he withdrew before sliding in with two. "Oh, Gabe."

"Yes, baby?"

"Oh my, I—" The orgasm hit her completely by surprise with enough power to make her body go limp.

Gabe released her nipple, kissing his way back up her body. When he reached her lips, he gave her the smile that made her fall for him in the first place. He reached for the condom he'd tossed onto the bedside table and made quick work of the foil and latex. When he settled against her again, Elina reached for him. Needing so much more than she thought she could want from him. From anyone.

He held the tip of his erection against her opening, and Elina's lids fluttered closed. Inch by inch, as he filled her, the electric currents of need and desire crackled around her. She bit her lip to keep from crying out and begging him to keep touching her.

"Look at me, sweetheart."

Elina forced her eyes open and gazed up at him, and he flashed a grin. Some sensation squeezed her heart and Elina tried desperately to get a handle on her emotions. But it was too late for that, because he started to move.

Gabe's hands fisted in her hair as he made love to her. The sweat dripping off his forehead, her body covered in a thin sheen. His hand gripping and tightening one moment, and soothing and massaging the next.

Her body arching into his, his driving into her as he whispered into her ear…

"Gabe."

"I have you, sweetheart."

And he did. Every bunched muscle. Every quirk of his lips or soft kiss. The tight grip on her hip and the fist in her hair. As they made love, she knew what he was telling her with his body but not those beautiful sculpted lips.

The trembling started in her toes, then shot through her body, lightning-quick and laying waste to her emotions like a tornado. While Elina's body pulsed and quaked, she fell in love with Gabe Alexander, and it terrified her.

With his lips on hers and stroking deep, Gabe shook above her, finally letting go with her pulsing around him.

Chapter 12

Gabe had Elina on the brain. Somehow she was able to be cool and professional. Distant, even. He'd stayed the night. They'd made love again...twice. But this morning, before he left, she'd been...distant.

Things were finally starting to progress for him, and all he could think about was her. Last night, if possible, was even hotter than the night on the yacht.

She was responsive and beautiful, and he didn't want to let her go. They needed to take it slowly; otherwise he was going to spook her. And he didn't want her running again.

The problem was now all he could think about was last night. Okay, the three times last night... But so far this morning, she was cool at best.

He didn't have time for this. He finally had a sit-down with Breckenridge Studios as well as one of their financiers, and he had to keep his head in the game. He had a job to do, and lusting after Elina Sinclair wasn't it. Although if that *was* a possible job description, then he'd be in line for promotion.

Delilah had assigned Elina to accompany him to the meeting and make sure he had everything he needed.

When the car service picked them up, she was all business. In the cab ride on the way over, once they pulled away from D. Donovan, he leaned over for a kiss and she shook her head. "You can't show up for your meeting with ruby lipstick all over your face."

She had a point, but he was still irritated, like an addict in need of a quick hit to get him through the day.

She finally leaned over, smiling sweetly, "Do you want this, Gabe?"

He scowled. "You know I do."

"Good. So spend less time focusing on my boobs and more time focusing on your script and your pitch. It's showtime."

And now that they were here, she was busy prattling on about who he was meeting with and what to make sure to say.

He knew what to say. He didn't need her telling him. *Easy, Alexander. She's just doing her job.* But a part of him wanted her to do less of her job and more of focusing on him. Of course that was stupid. But how could she be unfazed about what happened last night?

Once they were seated in the offices across from Julian Morte, the studio VP, and Colby Jakes, the financier, he couldn't keep his thoughts together. The beginning of his pitch was disjointed and sloppy.

But at one point, he met her gaze and she nodded her encouragement. She believed in him and this movie. That was just the jolt he needed. He managed to drag his focus back where it needed to be and away from Elina…and her boobs. And suddenly he was on. He walked the team through casting choices and why he'd made them. He even provided a CD of the recorded read-through for the execs to listen to on their own time. Once he got going, he settled into it. This was what he was meant to be doing.

The meeting ended on a high. When he was done, Julian leaned forward. "I'm extremely interested in what you've got here. I think we may have something." Everything was so close. So within his grasp. He could do this. He was going to get this movie made.

As they walked through the back hall toward the lot, he picked Elina up and swung her around. She giggled but smacked his arm. "Put me down. You need to compose yourself."

He couldn't help it. He was too excited. All the years of hard work and the last couple of weeks of torture working so closely with Elina, and it was finally paying off. Added bonus, he was finally alone with her.

"You, young lady, have been a bit chilly this morning."

She flushed and ducked her head. "I promise I haven't been." She sighed. "Or I don't mean to be. I—I've never done this before. And everything's about to get really busy."

He frowned. Yeah, busy. She was running.

"Okay. Say I buy that. I'm going to go ahead and demand my congratulatory kiss now. Then I'm going to ask you to talk to me. No more running. That was the deal."

Her gaze darted around. "Gabe, we are still on the studio lot. I promise you plenty of kisses when we get to my place later." She leaned away from him. "Or come to think of it, maybe we could go to your place. I can see where you live. Unless you have a wife and kid. And then that's extremely awkward."

She was deflecting. "Nope. The only woman I can handle is you." He had a better idea. He took her hand and tugged her down the hall. "Come on, I saw someone go down here."

She followed reluctantly. "Gabe, I don't think were supposed to be wandering around."

"Come on. Where's your sense of adventure? I know this isn't a yacht but I'm sure we can find—"

He stopped abruptly and then tugged her into a tiny office space, then locked the door. There wasn't much room, but it would have to do. "Alone at last." He pulled Elina close and held her there, letting the tension build. As always, she melted into him. "Now, I'll kiss you...as soon as I know what's wrong."

"Gabe, I—"

He pinned her with a direct glare. "Tell me."

She frowned, then blurted, "I'm scared."

Outside the door they heard rustling of keys, and she froze. When the key slipped into the lock, Gabe dragged her into the closet and closed them in.

"Are you serious right now?" she whispered. "We're going to get caught."

She was right. He was being careless. As if he hadn't just busted his ass to get money for his movie. "Just be quiet and stay still. In a minute we can leave."

She had him so wrapped up, he was willing to risk everything. This wasn't him. He wasn't normally so reckless. But then he didn't normally have a woman making him crazy.

Outside the door, someone was moving something around. In front of him, Elina squirmed. He felt every movement, every shift. And true to form, his dick was more than happy to let that continue. Idiot. "Elina. Stop moving."

"Sorry. Not like there's a lot of room in here," she whispered.

After several minutes of torture, she looked up at him, dark eyes bright and worried. Her voice was so soft, he could barely hear her. "I pulled back because I'm terrified of getting hurt. I'm frightened that I'll put myself out there, then I won't be able to commit, that I'll be just like her and ditch at the first sign of trouble. Or worse that I'll start to fall for you and you'll get bored. And—"

She was worried she'd hurt him. And she was worried he'd hurt her. He dipped his head and kissed her gently. He pulled back and her eyes were dazed and half-lidded. "Stop. No one is getting hurt, okay? We'll take this one step at a time, real easy. Casual," he whispered. He knew better than to tell her that he was already in love with her. And he knew she had feelings for him, too. Nope, he'd let her come to that conclusion on her own.

"I'm sorry," she mouthed.

He nodded acceptance of her apology, and glided his lips over hers again. It didn't take much with this girl. Her scent wrapped around him and he could hardly think. Barely string his thoughts together. She kissed him back, her tongue sliding over his, stroking, licking into his mouth.

The chant of need ricocheted in his skull. *Yes...faster... more...now...* Gabe gritted his teeth against the overwhelming need to take her. To brand her as his, so she would stop running, so she would understand how he felt.

He skimmed his hands up her torso, and her breath hitched as his thumbs caressed the underside of her breasts. *Yes, that's it.* Her body trusted him. Her body trusted itself. She just needed to let go and fall. Somewhere at the back of his mind, he registered that the person in the other room had left, and there was no more sound coming from outside, but he didn't want to break the spell. Locked in here away from everything else, she could talk to him, tell him what she was afraid of. He wasn't willing to let her go yet.

Elina moaned, arching her back into the caress. With her head tossed back, her eyes closed and her lips parted, she was the most beautiful thing he'd ever seen.

"Gabe," she whispered.

"Mmm?"

His brain was on vacation. No more thinking for him. What he wanted now was to touch her. To make her melt into a puddle in his arms. But he didn't want her retreating again. Not before he reminded her how good they could be together.

While he stroked one nipple into stiff alertness, he pulled up the fabric of her dress. Her hands gripped the lapels of his suit and she widened her stance. Yes. She wanted him as badly as he wanted her. She just needed some time to come around to see how great they could be together.

"Gabe, I just—I need…" Her voice trailed off as she writhed in his arms.

"I know what you need." She wasn't ready to hear about how he felt, but he could show her.

Her dress tugged up around her hips, Gabe slid his fingers under the hem of her panties.

Tearing his lips from hers, he kissed along her jaw and her throat. He knew her body so well now. Knew how to take her to the edge. Her breathing came in shallow bursts and he used his teeth, running them along her skin. "That's it, let go, sweetheart."

His fingers glided along the smooth skin of her wet folds and his legs shook. She was so wet. So ready for him. Sliding his fingers over her sensitive flesh, he relished her every cry and moan. Gently, he plucked at her stiff nipple, wishing he had room to take it into his mouth. He knew how sensitive her nipples were. How much she loved when he sucked on them, grazed them with his teeth.

With every slide of his fingers over her sex, he became less and less coherent. Her pleasure the sole focus of the only functioning brain cells he had.

His erection strained against his pants and he gritted his teeth against the pulsing, aching need. "Come for me, Elina. I want to feel you. I need to feel you." She rolled her hips onto his fingers and begged him with her body and her halted, muttered speech. And he delved a finger into her tight, sweet sex.

Gabe pulled back to watch her face. He loved nothing more to watch her as she flew apart. Elina's eyes went wide. And with a satisfied grin, Gabe ran his thumb over the tight bundle of nerves.

Just like that, his angel broke apart in his arms.

Her body limp against his, he released her breast and tucked her close. She might not know it yet, but he would fight to keep them together. She was his.

Chapter 13

"Elina, can you come in here for a minute?"

Elina swallowed hard as she pushed away from her desk. Oh shit. They knew. Delilah knew. Her body still hummed from her little studio adventure with Gabe. Willow must have sensed it. Why else would her boss call her in? *Oh, I don't know...to fire you from your job.* Elina should have known once...or twice...or three times with Gabe wouldn't be enough. And she was putting her job on the line. A job she loved. A job she worked hard for. *You. Are. An. Idiot.*

It wasn't like she could stop, though. *But you have to. Before anyone gets attached and hurt.* She promised him she wouldn't run. But there was no way they could sustain. She was going to end it...tonight. Okay, maybe tomorrow. One more for the road? Because it just felt good. She could still feel his hands all over her, making her tingle. *Get it together, Elina.* She grabbed her notebook and strode into Delilah's office with her chin up. "What's up, boss lady?"

Delilah's brows rose. "You're in a good mood. What's up with you?"

Shit. Way to overcompensate. "Huh? I'm good. Fine. Everything's perfectly okay. Nothing is up." Now would be a hell of a time to shut up.

Delilah narrowed her eyes and gave her a skeptical look. "If you say so. Am I working you too hard? You seem... on edge. You're sure nothing's going on?"

Elina shook her head. "Nope, everything is great. What can I do for you?"

"Well, I just wanted to say how impressed I am with the way you're handling Gabe."

Yeah, she was handling him all right. The memory of them in the closet at the studio made her flush and shift in her seat. "I'm—uh—grateful for the opportunity."

"Well, keep up the good work. Since the two of you are working so well together, I think I'm going to have you accompany him to Montreal next week."

Montreal? That would be amazing; so far, she'd only ever traveled locally for work. "Oh my gosh, that would be awesome." And then it struck her. She'd be alone... with Gabe. Complete unfettered access. There was no way they'd be able to keep their hands off each other. She bit back a groan. She couldn't go. Not if she wanted to stop the madness. "I'm super stoked to go, but isn't a trip like this meant for someone more senior?" It broke her heart to ask that question. But if she went to Montreal with Gabe, there would be nakedness. *Lots* of nakedness. She was weak. *Like your mother.*

"Yes, usually. But to be honest with you, the organizers will have someone on the ground. So all you have to do is make sure Gabe gets where he's supposed to be on time. It's a basic babysitting gig and not even that intensive. Think of it as a paid mini vacation. Do some sight-seeing. The city is beautiful."

There went *that* plan.

"Oh. Uh. If you're sure. I know Willow probably hasn't had a vacation in a while."

Delilah frowned. "Is there some reason you don't want to go? Has Gabe made you uncomfortable in any way?"

"No. Of course not. He's fine. A total professional." When they were working…when they were not working, however, he did this thing with his tongue. "I guess I'm afraid of screwing up. I know how important this is. But, new city, bright lights. Can't wait."

A slow smile crept over Delilah's pretty face. "Oh, how could I be so silly? You have a new boyfriend."

Elina practically choked on her own tongue as she sputtered. "No. No boyfriend. I swear. Not in a guy phase." Now, if only she could tell her body that. Because as far as her libido was concerned, when it came to Gabe Alexander, she was *absolutely* in a guy phase. More like a Gabe phase.

Delilah held up her hands. "Okay, you don't have to tell me. I know I'm just your boss. But I'm excited that you'll be doing something outside of the office. All you do is work, and it's not good for you."

Elina swallowed hard. She was a horrible liar, and she hated to lie to Delilah. "I promise, I don't have a boyfriend. But as soon as I do, I will tell you and you can stop worrying about me." There. Not technically a lie. Gabe was not her boyfriend. And they would stop…soon. Like after Montreal for sure.

"Okay. If you say so. Now go pack for Montreal. Summer is beautiful in the city."

"Sure thing." Great. It would be beautiful weather and she'd need to wear chain mail to keep herself from falling into Gabe's arms.

* * *

The way Gabe figured it, if he could just work out long enough and hard enough, he wouldn't obsess over Elina. *Easier said than done.* Because according to Delilah, they'd be traveling together next week. And that was a recipe for disaster. Too much too soon would spook her.

His phone rang in the living room, and he put down the weight to go and get it. As he jogged, the cool hardwood felt good against his feet. "Hello, this is Gabe."

"Gabe, this is Julian. I just wanted to say what a pleasure it was to meet you the other day. Your concept sounds amazing and we'd love to back this kind of picture for distribution."

Was this really happening? "Wow. Thank you."

"I understand you will be at the Montreal film festival."

"Yeah, that's right. I leave next week."

"Great. That's good. We'll be there, too. And we can follow up on some of the logistics. We'll need to lock up your talent and talk directors."

Everything was happening so fast he couldn't even believe it right now. "I'm definitely ready for another sit-down. So we'll plan to meet in Montreal, then?"

"Absolutely. And while we're there, there are a few people you should meet. I'll talk to your PR group to work that out."

"I look forward to sitting down with you again." When he hung up, he stared at his phone. Just like that, he had a backer for his movie. A mixture of joy and cold, stark fear flowed through his veins. Now that he had backing, he'd actually have to pull this off. He was up for the challenge. But it also terrified him.

His first instinct was to call Elina, but he hesitated. Would she be happy to hear from him? The waters were still muddy and he knew she was running scared. *You probably should've figured that out before you had your mouth all over her.* Screw it, he was calling her. He didn't want to play games.

She answered on the second ring and sounded wary. "Gabe? What's the matter?"

"Nothing. Actually everything is great. I just got a call from Julian. They've agreed to back to film."

She let out a loud whoop on the other end of the line. "Are you kidding me right now? That's awesome. I'm really happy for you." Then she added, "This is a cause for celebration. We'll get Willow and Delilah to expense it."

"You were the first one I called."

The line was silent for a beat, and he could practically hear her gears going. "So in Montreal, it's going to be a little crazy for you."

He could tell she was nervous about it. He might have a backer, but he still had a long way to go. And Delilah was worth her weight in gold. He was playing with his career. Why couldn't he leave Elina alone?

He knew the truth even if Elina didn't. If they couldn't keep their hands off each other when they were under pressure, there was no way they would keep their hands off each other in Montreal. Sooner or later, they would have to address exactly what they were doing.

But for now, he was content to talk and make her laugh. Because somehow talking to Elina made the good news feel ten times better.

Chapter 14

This was too easy. Being with Gabe. The moment they landed at Montréal-Trudeau airport, it was as if they'd been transported to some medieval city. The architecture featured Gothic and fanciful elements. Their hotel was stunning with the old-world European feel. And she was thrilled she was getting a chance to practice all her French.

After a day of meetings for him and shopping for her, he took her to dinner. "I probably should have mentioned earlier, but you look beautiful tonight."

Elina flushed and ducked her head. "Are you attempting to spit game at me now?"

Gabe laughed. "Game? What game? That first day we met, I was giving you all my best lines, but none of them worked."

"Yeah, well, that first day I was trying to stay far away from trouble. And you, sir, had a big old 'trouble lives here' sign on your forehead."

He grinned. "Hey, I resemble that remark."

"Yes, yes, you do." She leaned back in her chair. "Oh my God. If I eat any more French food, I am going to explode."

He laughed. "No one told you to eat that last bite of crème brûlée."

"But you were leaving that bite just sitting there on your plate. Come on. Didn't anyone ever tell you to finish your dessert?"

"I'm not sure that's a thing."

She laughed and nodded. "Yep, it sure is. Come on. Let's head back. I think I need to walk some of this off."

As they walked, he told her stories about growing up on sets. And the trouble he'd gotten into. He even told her about his first love.

"How old were you?"

Gabe grinned. "I was the ripe old age of ten." He trailed his fingers down her arm, then interlaced them with hers. "She was an older woman, you see."

"Oh really? Who was cradle-robbing the ten-year-old?"

"Her name was Jameson Parker, and she was eleven and played my on-screen sister."

"Oh my gosh. How scandalous of you."

"You can joke and mock all you like, but she was my first kiss. And we lasted two whole weeks."

"Well, look at you, starting young."

As his thumb caressed her fingers, he asked softly, "What about you? Who was your first love?"

Elina scratched at her nose. "I thought I was in love once. He told me he was, too. You know, the whole we'll-be-together-forever thing. Even had me briefly considering marriage after we graduated. Turned out, he wasn't really into forever. With Mom and everything, I figured I was better off on my own. I've always been a little afraid of love. I saw how crazy it made her. And then what happened to me…" Her voice trailed.

"I think that's sad."

She shrugged away his consideration. "No. Not sad. Maybe one day I'll fall in love and it'll hit me like a ton of bricks."

"Or maybe you won't even know it's happening to you," he added softly. What was he saying?

The prickle of awareness chased up her spine and tingled. "Gabe, what are we doing?"

"Relax, Elina. We're having fun and taking advantage of the fact that we don't have to hide and pretend that we're not crazy for each other right now. But it's totally no pressure."

But Elina knew it for what it was. This wasn't just a onetime thing or a six- or seven-time thing. Something fun for the moment. He was worming his way into her heart. Soon, his campaign would be over, and then what? It wasn't like she could tell herself not to feel. She had to protect herself so it didn't hurt too bad when he left.

Gabe was so in love with her. It should have terrified him. *Should've* had him running for the hills. Instead, he just wanted to hold Elina as close as she would let him.

Over the course of three days, they explored the city of Montreal, even taking a day trip over to Quebec. They'd done all the things that tourists and lovers do. And they had a great time doing it. She'd been completely affectionate and open with her touches and her heart.

And every night, they'd scorched the sheets. Sometimes they blistered the sheets in the morning, too…or the afternoon…well, anytime, really. And sometimes it had been the shower, the backseat of their rental car… He couldn't keep his hands off of her.

He'd known he wanted something more from her for weeks now, but this trip forced it. He was tired of giving her time to figure it out. This afternoon, she'd been busy eating an ice cream cone and ice cream dribbled on her chin. He kissed away the sticky sweet cream. And she'd smiled at him with the light in her eyes. He knew better than to tell her. She would only freak out, so he needed the perfect time and the perfect place. It was obvious she wanted him. But his patience was fraying under the weight.

The only real problem was what would happen with Delilah. He'd made her a promise, then broken it as soon as he'd seen Elina. They'd have to tell her the truth before it came out.

Because as much fun as it was sneaking around, he wanted to be with Elina in public. Montreal showed them how it could be. No more dragging her into alleyways or closets to kiss her. He wanted more from her. And to get that, they'd have to come clean to Delilah. Though that was easier said than done.

Chapter 15

The morning after their return from Montreal, Reece's phone rang and she answered grumpily. "Dude, where have you been? I've been texting and calling you for days, as soon as we got back from our honeymoon."

Elina held the phone away from her ear for a moment. When Reece worried, she tended to get loud. "Sorry, I've been out of town for last few days working on Gabe's campaign." Guilt seeped into her pores. This was Reece.

There was a beat of silence. "Gabe? As in Adam's Gabe? As in Gabe, Gabe?"

Elina scratched her nose. "Yeah, turns out he was my bright shiny new client."

"Oh goodness, Elina, this would only happen to you."

"Don't I know it. You can imagine my surprise when I walked into my meeting and there he was sitting there in all his gorgeous glory."

"What did you do? Did you tell your boss?"

"Are you kidding? There is no way I was telling Delilah. We just pretended we didn't know each other."

"And how has that worked out exactly?"

Damn Reece and her rational thinking. "Fine. It worked out fine. No big deal."

"Elina Sinclair, I know when you're lying. Don't make me call my mama to come get you."

Elina laughed. "Oh no, not Mama." Reece's mother had a way of delivering a verbal ass-whooping that stung worse than any spanking. "It turned out fine. It was a hard few weeks learning to adjust around each other, but we figured out a rhythm."

Her best friend laughed out loud. "And by rhythm, you mean who's on top in the bedroom?"

"Reece!"

"What? Are you really going to pretend the two of you aren't hot for each other? I can hear it in your voice. It's the way you say his name."

Elina covered her eyes and fell back in bed. "Do you think everyone knows?"

"Relax, I'm your best friend. I've known you since we were little. Delilah probably doesn't know. But what are you guys going to do?"

That was the question she'd been dreading since picking up the phone. "I don't know. We're just having fun. It's not like we can't stop." *Liar.*

"Fun," Reece said the word slowly as if she was talking to an imbecile. "So, you two were just having good times where no one will get hurt?"

Maybe Reece did understand. "Exactly. It's not serious. We can walk away anytime." She ignored the twinge of pain that accompanied the thought.

"Uh-huh. Let me ask, just how do you think this is going to work out for you? Sure you date plenty, but you don't really have that much experience with long-term boyfriends. I don't want to see you get hurt."

"Then good thing he's not my boyfriend." The truth of her friend's words rang her head. She didn't want to talk about Gabe anymore, so she dropped the other bomb instead. "So, Mom is getting married again. This time to her yogi."

Reece was silent, then cursed under her breath. "Oh man. Elina, I'm sorry."

"No, it's fine," she lied. "I learned to find that Zen place of my mother's. At least for a little bit. I sort of get her. Since I am acting out of control and impetuous I completely get how she can do it."

Reece sighed. "Elina, you are not your mother. You know that, don't you? Her mistakes aren't your mistakes. I'm worried about you with Gabe, but not because I don't think you guys wouldn't be great together. I worry you'll close yourself off to real feelings for him and get hurt in the process."

Elina swallowed hard, then for the first time, admitted her feelings out loud. "Reece, I have no idea what I'm doing. I'm lying to my boss. I'm sneaking around. This isn't me. I'm completely out of control. I don't know what to do with these feelings and it terrifies me."

"Honey." Reece's voice was gentle. "That's called falling in love. And what you do about it is, you talk to Gabe and tell him. Then the two of you figure out how to tell Delilah together."

She knew Reece was right. But that wasn't a decision she was ready to make yet. After all, what if he didn't feel the same?

Chapter 16

Elina adjusted her clothing for the third time as she stood in front of Gabe's door. *This is stupid.* Why was she so nervous? It was just him. She'd seen him yesterday. They'd made love yesterday...and this morning. What was so different about right now?

Well, for starters it was the first time at his place. So that was significant. And also, she was embracing her feelings. Also *significant.*

Suck it up, Elina, and get it done. They needed this talk. She knocked on the door three times, and it took a moment for him to answer.

Except when the door opened, it wasn't Gabe on the other side. It was a pretty blonde from the casting video. "Hi," she said. "Can I help you?"

Could she help her? Elina's mind worked through all the possible scenarios. She was here for a date. What was this girl doing here? "Yeah, I'm here to see Gabe."

The pretty blonde didn't move out of the way, but her gaze flickered toward the interior. "He's a bit busy right now. You want to leave a message?"

White-hot jealous fury flowed through Elina's veins. Leave a message? With this girl? She was standing here, concerned about how to tell Gabe that she'd gone and fallen in love, and this girl was trying to take a message for *him*?

Elina cocked her head and put on her best resting bitch face. "What's he busy doing?"

Blondie didn't budge. "He's in the shower. I'm sure he doesn't want me to let some random girl in here. He gets a lot of groupies from his earlier work. If you just leave me a message I'll make sure he gets it."

Something about the way the girl pinched her nose made Elina think that her message would go straight to the trash. And why did he need a shower? She had dealt with girls like this before. Privileged, who thought the world owed them something. "You know what, I'll wait."

Blondie frowned, as if confused as to why her ploy hadn't worked. From somewhere in the apartment Gabe's voice rang out. "Hey, Jacinda, I think it's almost seven so my next appointment is going to be here. We better wrap up. I need to get ready. Do you have any more parts of the script you want to review?"

The blonde flushed a deep shade of red and Elina smiled. *I got your number, honey.* "Gabe, I'm here early. Is that okay?"

He jogged over to the foyer with a wide grin. His hair wasn't wet. So much for a shower. The girl hadn't even been slick. "Hey, Elina. I see you met Jacinda. We're going over the script."

Elina strolled in past Jacinda and gave him a quick hug

before turning her attention on the interloper. "Oh yeah, we just met. I'm excited to see what you guys came up with."

Jacinda gave her a smile that was all teeth. "Actually, if you guys aren't going anywhere right now, I'd still like to go over a couple more things."

From Gabe's stance, Elina knew he was waffling. And she even understood why. He'd worked hard to get here, and he wanted it to be right. She wanted Jacinda gone, but she could be patient. "You guys go ahead. I'll just snoop."

The blonde smiled up at Gabe. "Okay, and we can talk about where you're going to take me out on Friday."

What in the world? Elina blinked at the two of them, not sure if she'd heard correctly. Had that woman just asked him out? In front of her?

Gabe was just as surprised as Elina was. He stammered at first, but then he recovered enough to say, "I, uh. Wow. Sorry, Jacinda, I'm seeing someone. Besides, I really want to keep the focus on the movie."

For a second Elina thought Jacinda whatever-her-name-was might pitch a fit, but then she smiled sweetly at Gabe. "Oh, I had no idea. What a lucky girl."

Elina could only agree. "Yeah, what a very, very lucky girl. I hope she knows the kind of guy she has."

Jacinda headed down the hall and Gabe pinned a look on Elina. "I am so sor—"

She put up a hand. "Don't worry about it. Go. Get this done. We'll hang out in a minute."

Gabe visibly relaxed. His grin flashing before he leaned down and kissed her properly. With just enough heat to make her knees go weak. "You're a star. We'll be done in thirty minutes."

Jacinda might've gotten what she wanted—to stay longer—but with that kiss, Gabe had left no doubt as to where she stood in his life. *Advantage Elina.*

* * *

Elina might be acting normal, but something was off. Gabe watched her carefully. She chatted excitedly about her new client and about Reece's return. But she didn't exactly meet his gaze. Was she pissed about Jacinda? He felt bad for going into overtime with her. But he wanted to make sure she was ready for the producer meeting.

He opened a fortune cookie and handed her the fortune before asking. "Are you pissed at me? You can tell me if you are. I know I should've told her to go."

She shook her head. "No. You're okay. She wasn't very nice, but I can handle girls like that."

He frowned and sat up. "What do you mean she wasn't very nice? You said she'd been keeping you company."

She rolled her eyes. "That was girl code for she wouldn't let me in the door and tried to get me to leave you a message."

He frowned. "She did what? But that's ridiculous—she knew you were coming over. I told her."

"And that was homegirl trying to sabotage me. Come on, Gabe, you have to know she's interested in you. It's obvious." She gestured to him. "There is the obvious packaging. With the smile and the eyes and whatnot. But now you're the filmmaker and this is your project. You're the executive producer. And that's very appealing to a lot of women."

Gabe flushed. He was an idiot. Jacinda had been dropping hints that she would be available to him *anytime*, when she arrived. But from the beginning he made it clear that he wasn't interested and that he had a date coming. *You have to make it even more clear, apparently.* The only woman he was interested in at the moment was sitting in front of him. "Just ignore her."

"Well, not exactly that easy to do. Women flock to you."

He perked up. This is the first inkling she'd ever given that she wanted to take things further with them. "Elina, are you jealous?"

She flushed and covered her face. "I swear I am not that jealous, bitchy girlfriend type. I don't know what's wrong with me. But it *bugged* me to see her here. It *bugs* me that she's been here all *alone* with you. And I understand that you were working on the script. That's the logical, rational part of my brain. There's a whole other part that wants to tear her head off."

"Elina, whatever you need from me I'll do. But first, I'm going to need you to say that this, what we have, is real for you, too. It's been real for me since the day I saw you in the Hamptons laughing at something Reece said. You were so damn beautiful, I couldn't take my eyes off you. We're seeing where this goes? Giving it a real try?"

Her eyes misted over and he worried he'd said something wrong.

"I'm afraid." Her voice was soft when she spoke.

"Baby, you don't have to be afraid. I'm not going to hurt you. You can do this if you want to. We can do this."

"I'm not sure how this happened. One day we were having fun. And the next, I'm acting like a jealous maniac in your apartment."

"You know as jealous maniacs go, I've seen worse." She swatted his arm. "Ow. Just kidding." *Not really.* "So now we can stop pretending that this is just temporary?"

She nodded as she sobbed. "Sorry about that. I just thought maybe you'd get bored and walk away, or I'd be able to hold my feelings separate from you, but I can't. It terrifies me."

"If it makes you feel better, it's a little scary for me, too. We'll figure it out together. The first thing on the agenda, though, we need to talk to Delilah before this gets way out of hand."

She groaned. "I know. I've been dreading that probability for a week now."

It might be unpleasant, but if it meant he got to hold on to Elina and keep his career, then he'd do it.

Chapter 17

Gabe nuzzled Elina's hair and inhaled the scent of her honeysuckle shampoo. He kissed her shoulder, and she nuzzled back into him. And of course his dick, nestled against her soft curves, twitched in response. She was so damn sexy. And she was *his*.

They needed to talk with Delilah today. And it wasn't going to be easy. He didn't want to impact Elina's job, but the only way to move forward was to be open and honest about everything. Delilah might be pissed, but Elina was a hard worker and really good at her job, so it was unlikely the consequences would be too stiff for her.

He, on the other hand, might be a different story. Delilah had been clear with him at the beginning. And he still needed her. He may have a producer and some investors onboard, but it never hurt to have the right kind of PR people in his corner. He wouldn't be where he was without her. He would hate to lose her as part of his team. *You should've thought about that before you touched Elina again.*

Yeah, well, he and Elina were sort of established before he signed on with Delilah, so he hoped that would count for something...

His phone buzzed on the nightstand, and he ignored it. He wasn't willing to let the real world intrude yet. Instead he kissed Elina's shoulder. "Good morning, sweetheart. Are you awake?" He kissed her again in the hopes of getting her to roll over.

"Mmm, I'm still sleeping," she grumbled.

"I promise you a surprise."

She pulled the sheets over her head and giggled. "Is this the same surprise that's been poking me for the last thirty minutes? Because if that's my surprise, then I might be inclined to turn around."

So she'd been awake. Deliberately trying to entice him. "So you knew he was missing you this whole time?" Gabe cupped her breast, slowly circling his thumb over her nipple, and Elina moaned under the caress. "As surprises go, I think this is one of my worst-kept secrets."

She rolled over and kissed him. "I would have to say so."

Elina slid a hand into his hair and scored her nails on his scalp, making him shiver. He kissed her deep, rolling her over so he was on top. When he drew back, he met her gaze. "I just want to make sure last night wasn't a dream. We're doing this, right? You and me?"

Her smile was soft, and she didn't shy away.

"Yeah, we're doing this."

He bent his head to kiss her again, but just before their lips touched, his phone rang again. Next her phone started to ring, and she frowned.

"Isn't it too early to start getting called in to work?" she muttered."

She was right. It was only six thirty. "Ignore it. I've been doing that with my phone for the last thirty minutes. It's probably your mother anyway."

Their phones both rang again, and Elina set up. "No, I think this is important." She reached over to the night-stand and unplugged her charger. "It's Delilah. I have to take this."

With a groan, Gabe rolled over and dragged the sheets over his lap. "That's fine, I'll just sit here, wondering what happened to my awesome wake-up call."

She swatted him before she answered. "Morning, Deli-lah, what's the matter?" In a second, she went from happy and relaxed to stiff and tense. "What? I don't understand. I—I'll be right in."

His phone buzzed again, and this time he picked it up. There were two urgent texts from Delilah, and one from Willow, calling him in to the offices ASAP. *Shit.* What was wrong? He slid his gaze up to Elina. "What's the matter?"

She dropped her phone on the bed and wrapped the sheets around herself. Grabbing the remote control she quickly turned the TV to the entertainment news channel. His picture was heavily prominent. As was one of Jacinda leaving his apartment last night, and one of him and Elina in Montreal, kissing.

Aw hell, the cat was out of the bag.

Chapter 18

"Elina, I expect better from you. What is the one rule we have here?"

Elina shifted in her shoes. She'd never seen Delilah so pissed in her life. "Startling honesty," she mumbled. She didn't even dare slide a glance over at Gabe.

"And when you walked into the conference room a few weeks ago, and you saw Gabe, you didn't think it was a good idea to tell me you already knew him?'

Gabe tried to jump in for an assist. "Look, this is my fault. I should've told you that we were involved, but when I signed the contract I didn't know Elina worked for you. Obviously she was worried about her job, and I was concerned that you would drop me as a client, so I asked her not to say anything."

Delilah rounded on Gabe and crossed her arms, tapping her foot, staring him down. "You seriously want me to believe that?"

Elina shook her head at him. "Gabe, stop." She turned back to Delilah. "This isn't his fault. *I* lied. I should have come straight to you. But I panicked. I met Gabe at the wedding. I never expected to see him again. And then he was here, and we were working together, and things just happened and I'm sorry. But this isn't his fault. He's got a great film and deserves to have it made."

Delilah lowered herself into her seat and clasped her hands together. From the corner of the room in the big leather chair, Willow sat lounging, but didn't move. She didn't even say a word. When Delilah spoke, her voice was icy. "Do you know why it's important that we don't sleep with clients?"

Elina nodded. "It's a conflict of interest, I know. Things like this morning with this company in the media for the wrong reasons. And I'm an adult, I made my decisions, and I will accept the consequences. I'm ready to do whatever it takes to handle the media."

Delilah sighed. "Elina, you show such promise. Why would you do this? You had a million times to come clean, to tell us. I'm here to help you. I've been you. You know how Nate and I got together. The media scrutiny almost killed me. That's why I put the rule in place so that something like this didn't happen. We needed to be aboveboard and now we've got a scandal with your name in the paper."

She'd royally screwed up and she knew it. *You should have just told the truth.* Instead, she wanted to prove herself so bad. She'd also wanted Gabe more than she wanted anything in her life. "Delilah, this job means the world to me. I am so sorry."

But Gabe didn't let her continue. "No, I'm sorry. We were coming to tell you today. We didn't think anyone saw us in Montreal, but neither one of us wanted to hide the truth from you anymore."

"Well, it's too late for that now isn't it, Gabe? When did you two make this little decision to tell me?"

If she'd told Delilah immediately, she wouldn't have worked so closely with him and she wouldn't have fallen in love. But now everything was so twisted she couldn't see a way out.

He cleared his throat. "Last night. We were going to tell you today."

Delilah narrowed her eyes. "So, what you're telling me is that, instead of calling me last night, after you made your little decision to, I don't know, be in love or whatever, instead of calling me right away, you waited. And now we have a media circus. Do either one of you want to tell me why Jacinda Johnson, your lead actress, was in your apartment? There are reports from a source close to her saying she's brokenhearted."

Gabe ran a hand through his hair. "We were working last night when Elina came over."

"This just keeps getting better and better." Delilah sat back in her seat. "We need to get in front of the media circus."

Elina sat up straight and squared her shoulders. This was one thing she could do. She could work this. She was good at this. "Okay, what do you need me to do?"

"You?" Delilah shook her head vehemently. "No. You are not doing anything, except staying out of sight. No work. No hanging out with your friends for the next couple days. Stay out of sight. Stay indoors. I don't want some paparazzo figuring out where you live and thinking he can get an exclusive story."

"But I'm part of the team. I need to do something."

"Right now, you're not part of the team. Right now, you're a client. So you need to act like a client whose face is on the bull's-eye."

"This is my job." She forced down tears.

Delilah blinked at her. From the corner, Willow chuffed and muttered, "Right about now, Elina, you need to consider yourself on probation. We need to fix this first, then we can talk about your job."

Elina's skin went clammy cold and her head swam. It was only when her head spun that she realized she'd been holding her breath. She released it, and her vision cleared. Her feelings for him were going to cost her her job. How the hell had this happened to her? When she met him she'd been on the verge of a promotion; her career had been taking off. And now she was media fodder and her job was on the line. All because she'd fallen in love and broken her own rules.

Delilah turned her attention to Gabe as Elina started to hyperventilate. "And you. I don't know what to say to you. The last month we have been working with you, keeping everything aboveboard, shedding that former image. And not only do you sleep with one of my staff, you put yourself in a precarious situation having the paparazzi catch Jacinda at your place."

Gabe shook his head. "Nothing happened with Jacinda. We were working."

"And I told you a million times, it's all about the perception. If you want to have a meeting with a beautiful, young costar of yours, do it at a restaurant. Preferably with outdoor seating. Or schedule a meeting in the studio or a neutral location. *Not at your house.* I was clear with you. And now we're in this situation. I would love to drop you as a client, but I'm afraid of how that's going to impact Elina."

"I'm not going to apologize for falling in love with Elina." His voice was soft but firm. "We should have been up-front. And like I said, I take full responsibility for that.

But I love her, so you're going to need to figure out a way around this."

Elina couldn't breathe. "Gabe, stop. Just stop. This isn't what I want. You've jeopardized your career. And I clearly put mine in danger."

He reached for her, but she pulled free. "I'm sorry, I can't do any of this right now." Before Willow could stop her, she turned to the redhead. "Don't worry, I'm taking the back exit, and I'll take a taxi."

As she ran out of the office, she could hear Gabe's footsteps behind her, but she ignored his calls and jumped into the first cab she saw with no clue where she was going or what she was doing.

Chapter 19

It had been a long two days for Gabe. Delilah had given him strict instructions to stay out of sight. But today he'd gone to the gym. On the way back to his place, he'd already gotten calls from the producer, who wanted to know what the hell was going on. According to him, the investor was nervous, given the negative press.

Gabe spent an hour calming him down, only to have several more phone calls from the casting office and his location scout concerned that the project was going to be shelved.

He'd tried to call Elina several times. But she didn't answer. Fuck, how did things get so bad? After Elina, he tried calling Jacinda. She took his call immediately. "Oh my God, Gabe, I had nothing to do with this. I swear."

He wasn't sure if he should believe her or not. From what Elina said, he wouldn't put it past her, down to the paparazzi sighting. He chose his words carefully. "Jacinda,

I'm not sure what happened, but we need to get it under control. I've got photographers camped out on my doorstep."

"I know. Me, too. I had no idea they'd be waiting outside your place. So what do we do?"

And this was the tricky part. He and Delilah had discussed his options.

He understood Jacinda would want to capitalize on this for long as possible. There was no way he was going to work with her on the phone; this was her doing. So they made an appointment to meet at Delilah's office tomorrow.

After a day of going stir-crazy and trying to find Elina, his phone rang. He dived for it, hoping it would be her; it was Adam. "Dude? Where the hell have you been?"

"I've had my phone bombarded by media. So I haven't been answering."

"Reece is all over my ass. She wants to know what the hell is going on. And she wants to know where Elina is."

"I wish I knew where Elina was. She won't take my calls right now. And as far as what's happening, my life is a circus. Thanks to Montreal and Jacinda."

"Man, I could've told you that. Jacinda? That chick is trouble with a capital *T*. You can take one look at her and know that. She's a social climber. She will do just about anything or anyone to be famous."

How did he miss that? He quickly filled Adam in on how things had blown up. "Yeah," Gabe said. "Been a rough couple of days."

"So what are you going to do?"

"I don't have many other options but to wait for Elina to realize that I'll still love her when she comes back from wherever it is she's gone."

Chapter 20

"It's not just the tabloids, Mom. Gabe and I, we don't work together."

Her mother dismissed her with a wave of her hand. "What are you talking about? That's nonsense. No couples just *happen*, you have to work and fight hard even when you don't think it's worth fighting for, you tell me that all the time. I happen to love that new-couple feeling. That's what *I* do. Not what *you* do. In so many ways, you're more grown-up. That's who you are. You deal with things. So what are you doing here in Toronto, like someone who ran away from her life?"

"Delilah said to lie low. I'm lying low." Elina slammed down her glass. "If you don't want me here and you want to have your love nest with yogi or whatever, I'll go."

The early-morning sunlight was pouring in the floor-to-ceiling windows. The view from her mother's loft was beautiful. She'd always loved this place. She'd grown up in upstate New York, but as soon as she was off to boarding school, her mother had moved to Toronto.

"You know full well I don't want you to go. I love having you here. But I don't love you moping. You can talk to me if you want." Her mother eased herself down onto the couch.

"I don't want to talk about it. You never said how much this would hurt. You always talk about love like it's this beautiful, magical fairyland. This is real talk. It hurts like hell. I would like it to stop. I want to stop thinking about him. I want to stop loving him. I want to stop missing his arms around me when I sleep. I want it to stop because it is interfering with my life."

"Oh, honey, but that's love. It's not clean and analytical. It's messy and emotional, but pretty great if you let it happen."

"Getting involved with him has turned my life upside down. My emotions are out of whack. I'm on the verge of being fired from my job. It's not worth it. I want everything to go back to normal. I'm throwing everything away because of what? Some guy? When another one could just come along in six months?" But she didn't want another guy. She wanted Gabe. And she didn't want to want him.

She stood and started to pace the length of the hallway. "I mean I finally got it. Why you were always chasing love. I got it because it was nice to wake up to someone who was going to be there and hold me. Someone to call when I was happy and encourage me and push me. But it came at costs I didn't really think about paying."

Her mother sighed. "Baby, I know I put you through the wringer with all of my marriages. In particular the one to your father. Or rather the several to your father... I know I was looking for something and am still looking for it. Your dad is the closest I've ever come. I'm looking for the

YOUR PARTICIPATION IS REQUESTED!

Dear Reader,

Since you are a lover of our books – we would like to get to know you!

Inside you will find a short Reader's Survey. Sharing your answers with us will help our editorial staff understand who you are and what activities you enjoy.

To thank you for your participation, we would like to send you 2 books and 2 gifts – **ABSOLUTELY FREE!**

Enjoy your gifts with our appreciation,

Pam Powers

SEE INSIDE FOR READER'S SURVEY

For Your Reading Pleasure...

We'll send you 2 books and 2 gifts
ABSOLUTELY FREE
just for completing our Reader's Survey!

YOUR READER'S SURVEY
"THANK YOU" FREE GIFTS INCLUDE:
- ▶ 2 FREE books
- ▶ 2 lovely surprise gifts

PLEASE FILL IN THE CIRCLES COMPLETELY TO RESPOND

1) What type of fiction books do you enjoy reading? (Check all that apply)
- ○ Suspense/Thrillers
- ○ Action/Adventure
- ○ Modern-day Romances
- ○ Historical Romance
- ○ Humor
- ○ Paranormal Romance

2) What attracted you most to the last fiction book you purchased on impulse?
- ○ The Title
- ○ The Cover
- ○ The Author
- ○ The Story

3) What is usually the greatest influencer when you <u>plan</u> to buy a book?
- ○ Advertising
- ○ Referral
- ○ Book Review

4) How often do you access the internet?
- ○ Daily
- ○ Weekly
- ○ Monthly
- ○ Rarely or never.

5) How many NEW paperback fiction novels have you purchased in the past 3 months?
- ○ 0 - 2
- ○ 3 - 6
- ○ 7 or more

YES!
I have completed the Reader's Survey. Please send me the 2 FREE books and 2 FREE gifts (gifts are worth about $10) for which I qualify. I understand that I am under no obligation to purchase any books, as explained on the back of this card.

168/368 XDL GKEX

FIRST NAME

LAST NAME

ADDRESS

APT.#

CITY

STATE/PROV.

ZIP/POSTAL CODE

K-816-SFF15

BUSINESS REPLY MAIL
FIRST-CLASS MAIL   PERMIT NO. 717   BUFFALO, NY

POSTAGE WILL BE PAID BY ADDRESSEE

READER SERVICE
PO BOX 1867
BUFFALO NY 14240-9952

NO POSTAGE
NECESSARY
IF MAILED
IN THE
UNITED STATES

◄ If offer card is missing write to: Reader Service, P.O. Box 1867, Buffalo, NY 14240-1867 or visit www.ReaderService.com ►

glimmer of hope I saw inside your dad when I first met him. It has led me down some dark paths."

"Sometimes I wish you guys stayed together. Not that second time, though. I was worried you might kill him. But that last time, I dunno, I thought maybe it would stick. Do you regret any of it, Mom?"

"Not a bit with your father. I got you, and you are the most important thing to ever happen to me. Every single one of the men I've married or been engaged to had something fantastic to offer. And I recognize it's my fault that you think love is a bad thing. I promise you it's not. It's only how I handle it that's a bad thing. I'm just not really good with my emotions most of the time. I never wanted that for you. But I did want you to find love and not be afraid of it."

"I'm not afraid of love. Mom, I'm afraid of turning into you. You've always been smart, and the most beautiful woman in the room. And yet you chased these men and chased these relationships. I wanted to be beautiful like you were and smart like you were. But I didn't want to depend on anyone for my happiness and well-being." She sniffed. "I guess that didn't work out so well."

Her mother pulled her in for a hug. "Sorry I hurt you, Elina. I never wanted to give you hang-ups about this stuff. My inability to find love has more to do with me and the men I've chosen than anything. The man you chose, he seems like a good man."

"You don't even know Gabe."

"I know he loves my daughter. I know that he's probably trying to do something with his life, and I know he is willing to let you breathe."

"What are you talking about? He's been pursuing me since the Hamptons. Letting me breathe put me in the line of falling-in-love fire. There's no woman who can resist him. And I'm one of them. I fell for the trap. And it hurts."

Her mother patted her hair. "Oh, my poor, sweet baby. Just one question. How do you feel about him?"

That was the question. And the truth stung. "Like part of me is going to die when I'm not with him."

"And what are you doing here with me? Seems like maybe you belong there. And you work it out together. Honey, there was never any danger of losing yourself in some guy. You're too tough for that. But you do need to leave yourself open to love to find true happiness. Can't run away from that part of yourself, either."

She knew her mother was right. She was miserable without him. And what she kept doing wasn't working, obviously. Avoiding love and relationships just to avoid getting hurt, and here she was. Hurt nonetheless. She just hoped there was still a way to save a relationship with Gabe *and* save her job. Because she was not a quitter.

Chapter 21

On Monday, Elina was back in the office. She'd taken a late flight out of Toronto the night before and made the ride home with very little fanfare. Her mail, of course, had stacked inside her door. She'd only skimmed through it this morning. Several of the paparazzo had left her notes requesting to chat with her. *Yeah, as if that was going happen.*

When she arrived, Delilah was already in the office. She heard the sound of heels clicking on the floor. When she knocked on her office door, Delilah looked up. "Elina, I didn't expect you back for another couple days."

"I know. And thank you for whatever you've done to take care of the media mess. But I couldn't sit and hide any longer. And I couldn't stand knowing that I really messed this up. You gave me a chance, and I'm grateful for that. I should never have lied to you and I know better. I panicked. I didn't know what to do and I panicked. I didn't plan on having feelings for him. They just *happened*."

Delilah sat back. "You remind me a lot of me. Super-driven. Always wanting to be able want to fix something, never saying die. It also makes you prone to closing yourself off." She sighed. "With a couple more days to think about it, I realize I probably came down a little hard on you. It's not like I wasn't ever in the same situation. But I won't lie, it was difficult for Nate, and I thought a guy like Gabe would mess you up. Given everything he's done this week, I guess I was wrong about him."

Elina frowned. "What did he do?"

Her boss's delicate brows drew up. "You haven't seen the news?"

"No, I got a flight from Toronto late last night and have been holed up inside my apartment. What's going on?"

"Despite my efforts, he spoke to Jacinda. Got her to give a statement that they were rehearsing the script."

"Yeah, but why would she do that? She's clearly into him."

"Well, apparently she's more into her career. And once she found out what was at stake, she was willing to play ball. I know what this job means to you and honestly, I don't want to lose you. But you've got to be honest with me from now on. I need to know that when something is going down, you'll tell me first."

With a giant breath of relief, Elina sagged. "So you're not going to fire me?"

"Not today. Not because you fell in love. I may have been wrong about him."

"I owe him an apology, too. I'll try to go by his place after work."

"Why don't you consider this one of your days off and go fix your life so tomorrow we can start fresh? You've got new to clients to deal with."

Chapter 22

Elina paced in front of Gabe's door. Back at the office she'd worked out what to say. And it went something like, "Hi, I was an idiot. I love you. Take me back." Except now that she was here, standing in front of his door, she didn't know how to do this.

She was in love. It had happened to her. The one thing she'd always said she didn't want. But now that she wanted it more badly than she'd ever wanted anything else in her life, she had no idea how to go about getting it. Or keeping it. Had she blown it? Would he still want her after she'd run? No man was that patient.

She turned to leave. This was a stupid idea. But then her mother's words rang in her head. "You're strong. You deal with things." And that halted her in her tracks. She could be strong. She could tell him that she loved him. What was the worst thing that could happen?

Oh, you know, he doesn't love you back? But she needed

to do this; otherwise, she'd be doing this her whole life. Just like her mother.

She turned back around and took a deep breath. As she fought her churning gut, she forced herself to stand strong. She was doing this. It would hurt, but she was going to do this.

Elina knocked.

Gabe peered through the peephole and his breath caught. Swinging the door open, he stared. She was there. She was okay. "Hi." He managed to swallow around the emotions welling in his throat.

She licked her lips, and his gaze focused on the tip of her pink tongue as she ran it over her lips. "Hi. Do you mind if I come in for a minute?"

"Not at all." Stepping aside to let her in, he took the opportunity to drink her in. Every strand of her hair, what she wore, how she moved. Everything. He knew why she was here. To end it. If he wasn't going to get to be with her again, he wanted to remember this moment. "I was worried about you."

In his living room, she turned to face him. "I'm sorry about that. I hit the boiling point and I needed to get out for a while."

She needed to run from him for a while, was what she really meant. He'd known this was eventually coming, but he hadn't been prepared for how much it would hurt. "Where'd you go?"

Elina rolled her lips inward. "To see my mom in Toronto."

He raised his eyebrows. That was a surprise. "Oh. Wedding stuff?"

She shook her head. "No. For once, me stuff. I needed to get my head on straight. And oddly going to Mom seemed like the right solution."

Gabe folded his arms. To keep from touching her. He needed to get this over with. "Elina, look—"

"Gabe, please, I—"

"I love you, Elina." The words came tumbling out before he could stop them. "I have been in love with you since that day on the yacht. Since the first day, actually, at the café. I knew you were special." He had zero control of his mouth right now. It was already out. Might as well finish it. "I know you care about me, but if you're not willing to try, then I need to leave you alone, because it's killing me. Every time you run, it carves a piece of my soul out. And I can't keep doing that to myself."

"Gabe, if you just—"

He interrupted her again in an effort to ward off the pain that was coming. If she didn't say the words, it wasn't real, right? "No, I can't. I can't just watch you walk away again. I can't just pretend that this is temporary. Every time we get close you bolt. And I—"

"I love you," she said quietly.

Gabe stared. "Excuse me?"

Her lips twitched. "I love you. That's what I've been trying to say, but you keep interrupting. I'm also trying to say I'm sorry for running, for not knowing that what I needed was right in front of me... I—"

Gabe's skin hummed with excitement and anticipation as he pulled her close, stopping her again with a kiss. "Damn, I missed you," he whispered against her lips.

Elina looped her arms around his neck. "I missed you, too. I can't promise you I won't be scared again, but I'm a fighter and I will fight for us. I finally know what I want, and it's to be with you."

Gabe nuzzled her nose with his. "Good, because my only plan was to pretty much keep kissing you until you realized you loved me."

Elina grinned up at him, and he saw his future in her eyes. She was his. "Sounds like a plan to me."

* * * * *

This book is for my baby brother Jonathan. Just because he never thought I would dedicate a book to him.

Dear Reader,

Costa Rica is a country that has captivated me since I saw pictures of the vacation my friend took there. Gorgeous beaches, colorful animals and lush rainforests that are so beautiful they seem unreal. Is there a better place to fall in love? I hope you enjoy reading Marcus and Willa's story as much I enjoyed writing it.

Jamie

SEDUCED BEFORE SUNRISE

Jamie Pope

Chapter 1

This place is like Fantasy Island, Willa Arthur thought as she stepped off the tiny plane that had brought her to a remote part of the country. Well, maybe not like Fantasy Island. There were no men in white suits with big smiles to greet her, and she was pretty sure her wildest dreams weren't about to come true. But she had nothing else to compare this experience to. She had never been to Costa Rica. She had never been anywhere really, except to central Florida to visit her grandparents in their retirement community. There she saw a lot of palm trees and in-ground pools. Billboards for places like Alligator Land and restaurants with all-you-can-eat buffets. As a child that had been infinitely cool to her. But this...

She looked around her in awe once again as her taxi took her to the resort. She finally understood what paradise was. It washed over her, and a sense of calm she hadn't felt before made her sink back in her seat and finally relax.

The ocean was on one side of her, and the jungle was on the other. White sand met thick green lushness, and she had to resist the urge to press her nose against the window like a small child and stare at it all. There were no high-rises like in her Manhattan neighborhood. No backed-up highways or honking horns. No fast-food chains or big-box stores littering the landscape. It was just beautiful, clean and quiet. It was like nothing else she had ever experienced before, and somehow it was too much for Willa in that moment. She shut her eyes and leaned back in the seat realizing that before this trip, she hadn't been more than a block from her apartment in the last month.

She needed to get out more.

More than down to the corner store to stock up on coffee and her daily supply of food. She had become a hermit as of late, or a writer on a deadline, as she liked to think of herself. She wrote mystery novels, bestsellers that were gritty and funny at the same time. Her parents hadn't been thrilled when she told them she was going to quit her well-paying job at the university to write full-time. But she didn't let her PhD in forensic science go to waste. Writing books helped her combine her loves of science and words. Though writing her books had also hurt her social life.

Big-time. She lived in New York City. The city that never sleeps. The city where on any given night there were thousands of people looking to make connections, yet she couldn't remember the last time she had a real conversation with anybody other than her editor. That's why she was glad this trip came along. Not just because she was happy to celebrate the wedding of one of her oldest friends, but also because she seriously needed to get out of the house. And get dressed every day. And remember how to carry on a conversation that wasn't about books and subplots and red herrings.

She was going to laugh, she told herself. And dance and have a good time celebrating Virginia's marriage. Or at least she was going to try real hard to. Even in her old job she didn't see many people. She had spent her days in a lab studying tissue samples and specimens, speaking only to the few other socially awkward biochemists.

This exotic wedding was a treat for her, her gift to herself for turning in her fifth novel.

"We're here, ma'am," her cabdriver said to her in perfect English.

"We're where?" She sat up and stared out the window expecting to see a large beach resort with a poolside bar and some cabanas, but all she saw was a jungle. Thick green trees with a tiny path that looked like it was cleared with just a machete.

"At your destination, ma'am," he said to her like she was dim.

"But—but this can't be it." She fumbled in her bag for the confirmation form. "Maybe I gave you the wrong address."

"You did not. This is it. The Divino Rain Forest Resort. It is very popular."

"Oh." She looked at the path again, and this time she saw the little wooden sign that marked the resort's entrance.

"It is an eco-friendly resort. The owners pride themselves on leaving as small of a footprint on the environment as possible."

"Oh," she said again, and the vision of the luxurious tropical vacation she had been looking forward to evaporated. It was replaced by images of tents, sleeping on the ground, cans of bug spray and campfire cooking.

She had barely been out of her house lately; she wasn't sure she could rough it in the jungle for the next five days.

Hell, she didn't even have any appropriate clothing for this adventure. She thought about the colorful assortment of sundresses she had in her bag and wondered if any of them could be turned into pants. Then she thought about telling the cabdriver to turn around and head back to the airport.

She could claim that bad weather in New York had delayed her flight, or that she had some kind of devastating stomach bug that could infect anyone she touched.

"Ma'am? Are you going to go in?"

She sighed. This was Virginia's wedding. And Virginia was her best friend. The only one who got her, who went to the library with her instead of school dances. The girl whose house she slept over at every weekend. The only friend she could spend hours with just talking about books and other nerdy things. She couldn't go back to New York.

She would never forgive herself for missing her best friend's wedding. She steeled herself. "I'm going in."

"You'll have a nice time," her driver reassured her as he got out to get her bag. She stepped out of the cab and onto the unpaved path that was the hotel's entrance.

To her surprise there was a little wooden house just beyond the trees. It was more like a large hut with a thatched roof, but as she got closer she could see how beautiful it was. The reddish-brown wood seemed to gleam in the sunlight that filtered through the trees. The windows were made of thick greenish glass and covered in lattice, and two tree trunks flanked the entryway. The railing on the small porch was intricately carved and looked handmade. It was clear some brilliant carpenter had made this little building look like it had been there for years, as if nature erected it.

"Welcome to Divino!" A man in a brown uniform came

out and greeted her. "You must be Ms. Arthur. We were expecting you."

"You were?" she asked dumbly. "I mean, yes. Thank you."

"Please allow us to take your bag to your room. There is another wedding guest waiting for the shuttle up to the resort. Let me show you to our Welcoming House."

She walked up to the room to find a very tall well-dressed man staring out the window at the side of the house. Even from behind she could tell he was attractive. Just by the way he held himself. His broad shoulders and hard-looking back seemed to take up all the space in the little waiting room. His smell did, too. Spicy and clean. Soapy. Not like some of the expensive cologne she smelled on men recently. She liked the smell, and combined with the clean Costa Rican air, the scent was slightly intoxicating. It made her want to inch a little closer and inhale deeper.

"Ms. Arthur, would you like some water before you head up to the resort?" the bellman asked, and at the same moment the stranger turned around to face her. Only he wasn't so strange. The air flew out of her lungs. She knew him. Well. She had thought he was beautiful inside and out when she was still a girl in high school, but he had changed in the fourteen years since she had laid eyes on him.

All the traces of boy she once knew were gone. Marcus Simpson—Marc as she had called him—was a man now. There was no softness to his face, no innocence. Just a hard jawline, chiseled features and beautiful milk-chocolate-brown skin. His hair was gone, too, replaced by a perfect bald head that very few men could pull off. He was more than beautiful now and he was looking at her directly in her eyes, like she was the only one in the world. He was looking at her the way he used to. The way no one else ever did. It used to make her feel special.

Now all she wanted to do was punch him in his handsome face.

Marc Simpson was the guy who'd obliterated her heart.

"Ma'am? Would you like some water?"

"Oh." The bellman's voice startled her. She was tempted to take the cup, to dump it over her head just to cool her overheated skin. Her face was burning, her chest, her heart. Her reaction to him was strong and unexpected. His presence there was unexpected. She hadn't seen him since the spring before she went off to college. She vowed never to be in the same room again, vowed never to be around anyone who made her feel small and unworthy. And yet there he was, staring at her with curious intensity. She couldn't take it. "No—no, thank you."

"If you don't want to wait for the shuttle you could walk up to the resort desk." The bellman's eyes narrowed as if he sensed her distress. "It's only about a ten-minute walk. Our shuttle is electric and as eco-friendly as possible, but we encourage our guests to walk the grounds and be one with nature as much as possible."

"That's a great idea." She turned for the door. "I'll walk." She needed to be out of that room, away from Marc and that suffocating feeling he brought along with him. She had been so in love with him that she didn't know which way was up. Seeing him now brought back memories. Brought her back to the moment when he humiliated her, to the moment when all of her confidence evaporated with a few cruel words from his lips.

"I'll walk, too," she heard him say as she left the room.

"Damn it," she grumbled, and sped up, trying to put as much distance between them as possible. She couldn't even think, knowing he was around. What was he doing here? It couldn't just be a coincidence. He just wouldn't happen to be at the same resort as her in a secluded part of the Costa Rican jungle. But then she remembered what the bellman said. There was another wedding guest waiting. That wedding guest was her high school sweetheart.

"Hey!" She heard his heavy footsteps behind her. "Wait up."

She ignored him, trying to walk faster even though she knew it was useless. Her short legs were no match for his long powerful ones.

"Damn, you move fast for a little thing." He came up beside her, grinning as if they were old friends just strolling together. His voice had changed, she noticed. That slight Southern accent he had when he moved to her neighborhood had all but disappeared. She was glad. She used to think his voice was sweet. He didn't deserve to have a voice like that anymore. There was nothing sweet about him. "The bellman said that this walk is supposed to take ten minutes, but with the way you're moving we'll be there in five."

She said nothing, just looked at him. He wasn't dressed for a trek through the jungle either, in his designer jeans, shirt and blazer. She desperately wished a large bird or monkey or whatever wild animals lived in these parts would drop a present on his pretty clothes.

"You're Willow, right?" he asked and the anger she was feeling turned right into a full-blown rage. He didn't remember her name? He had kissed her lips and whispered her name hundreds of times. He had made love to her. He had told he was in love with her.

And he didn't remember her name?

Maybe it wasn't rage she was feeling, it was stupidity. She felt stupid for pinning so many hopes on a guy who clearly thought very little of her.

She opened her mouth to let him have it, but he just went on talking, robbing her of the chance. "When I first pulled up here I was sure I had the wrong place. I had visions of those horror movies where they lure unsuspecting people to resorts, to perform weird experiments on them. For a while I was seriously worried about the state of my organs. Especially since I can't get my phone to work out here. That's why I was so glad to see you. It seems more legit now. And if it's not legit, at least I'll go missing with somebody I know from high school."

Somebody he knew from high school! Now she was just somebody he knew?

She stopped short, unable to take his stupid chatter any longer. "Shut up, Marc! Shut up! Shut up, shut up! I don't want to walk with you. I don't want to hear you ramble. I don't even want to lay eyes on you. Stay away from me!"

She walked ahead, leaving him standing there in silence.

"Why?" she heard from behind her. There was surprise in his deep voice.

"Why? Why?" She turned around, stopping in front of him. "Should I list the reasons? Number one, you don't even remember my name. Number two, you're an asshole. Number three—"

He grabbed her arm and pulled her close to him. She could feel the heat of his body, take in his clean soapy smell and really see into his eyes. All the traces of humor were gone. He was studying her intensely again, his eyes sweeping across her in such away she wanted to cover herself up, hide from his inspection.

She tried to yank herself away, but he wouldn't let her. He pulled her even closer, so that her chest brushed his. She hated herself for it, but her nipples tightened and those stupid tingles rushed along her skin and down her spine. She was too aware of him, too attracted to him. Still. She had hoped time and hatred would dull it, but they hadn't.

She still felt the same way she had when she was seventeen and she first felt his body against her.

"I know who you are, Willa Rose Arthur. Born in April. Scared of thunder and allergic to almonds. I know you very well." His accent was back, just a hint of it, and she remembered that it got thicker whenever he felt a stronger emotion.

"I guess I should be grateful that the super popular Marcus Simpson would remember a lowly nerd like me." She pulled herself away, and this time he let her go. She turned away from him, continuing her walk up to the resort.

If she wasn't feeling so many things she might have taken the time to notice how beautiful her surroundings were. How the air felt different. How she was truly in a place that was magical, but all she could think of was Marc. How he was silently walking behind her. How she could still feel him on her skin and how his scent lingered in her nose. How she was so angry at him when she promised herself that if she ever saw him again she would be icy cool.

She wasn't sure if she could spend the next five days near her former high school boyfriend. She was still too damn hurt.

But what could she do? Going home wasn't an option. She was here for her friend, and her friend had no idea what had gone on between them all those years ago. She wished she had told Virginia, but she couldn't at the time; her humiliation had been too deep.

"Of course I remember you, Willa," he said to her as the resort finally came into view. "It's hard to forget the girl you lost your virginity to."

Chapter 2

Willa came to a dead stop again like his admission shocked her. But she had to have known she was his first, just like he had known he had been hers. The awkward touches, those sweet, slow kisses, the closeness. He hadn't forgotten her.

How could he?

She slowly turned to face him, her mouth open slightly, and for some reason it brought those sweet, slow kisses they had shared right to the front of his mind. He should have been focused on apologizing for how horrible he had been to her when they were still kids, or how he was going to survive the next week with a woman who clearly hated him. But he couldn't think clearly. All he could do was stare at her. His little Willa had grown up. Those thick glasses she used to wear were gone, no longer hiding those big, pretty deep brown eyes he used to love looking into. She seemed to have grown taller, too, but he knew that was impossible, but she held herself differently, more confidently. Her body had always been delightfully curvy and soft to the touch, but only *he* had known that in their teenage days; now the world could see it, too. She wore a long green dress with a tropical print that looked damn good against her pretty brown skin. It skimmed her hips and clung slightly to her backside, and while he hated that she kept walking away from him, he didn't mind watching her leave. The sway of her hips was almost hypnotic. But now she was standing before him in a cleavage-baring summer dress with her pouty lips parted, and his mind was totally blank of coherent thoughts.

It brought him back to those days when all she had to do was smile at him to turn him on. He hadn't expected that. He had expected to feel nothing for her except a little lingering guilt, maybe a little fondness for the girl who had made him a man.

No, he hadn't forgotten her. He never would.

"Willa…"

She shook her head, disgust clear on her face. "I don't want to speak to you. I don't want to look at you. I don't even want to be in the same hemisphere as you."

"You can't still be this mad over something that happened when we were teenagers," he said, not knowing what else to say. He knew she was, though. He knew she had every right to be mad at him, because he was still mad at himself. He had hurt her.

"Don't tell me what I can or can't be. I can be mad at you if I want! You're not the boss of me."

What happened to his formerly super-quiet girl? Time had given her passion and heat. It made her downright pissed off. He wanted to smile at her outburst, but he knew better. She might knock him out if he did.

"I think we need to talk."

"Why?" Instead of seeing anger, he saw genuine hurt flash in her eyes. It was only there for a moment, but it was hard to miss. "I think you said everything you had to say when you publicly humiliated me in front of all your friends." She turned away from him, once again walking toward the resort.

This had gone completely wrong, one of the rare missteps in life. He had always been so cool under pressure. He never let anybody see him sweat, never let anyone see him out of control. It was why he was so good at his job. He worked in public relations, making dirty politicians look squeaky-clean. He had a solution for every problem, yet he had no idea what to do about Willa.

He followed her up the hill that led to the front door of the resort. He hated that he was feeling stupid, feeling unsure of himself. He was never unsure of himself. But now he felt the same as he did when he was fourteen and too tall and awkward for his age and body. He felt like he did when had just moved from South Carolina to New Jersey to live with his aunt and uncle. He shouldn't, though. He was a man now, and all that childhood BS was done and over with. He had moved on from his humble beginnings.

But you never moved on from Willa.

He shouldn't care that she was still mad at him. He had worked so hard to fit in in school, to be cool. To show the kids of that well-to-do town that he was more than that boy with the poor single mother and the slow accent who was good with a football and sometimes got angry for no reason. He had really thought he needed those guys then, that he needed his popularity. He was just a kid. She had to understand that. She knew him better than anybody else back in those days.

She was the only one who really knew him.

Shit.

He had to fix this, to really truly apologize so that he could move on. He could fix everyone else's mess. It was time to fix his own. And if she couldn't forgive him, at least he could forgive himself. Then maybe he would stop feeling like an out-of-control kid again.

He grabbed her arm, immediately feeling the little sizzle of heat when his hand connected with her smooth skin. Part of him wanted to take it away before he got burned. The other part of him wanted to put his other hand on her, to slide his fingers all over her tempting brown skin. Instead he spun her around so he could look into her eyes.

"We need to talk. We've got to put this behind us."

"If you don't stop grabbing me I'm going to kick you in your manhood."

Her threat tempted him to let go, but his hand had a hard time releasing her. "You know I'm not going to hurt you."

"Not physically maybe, but your words are lethal enough."

"Willa? Marc, is that you?" They both looked up to see Virginia, her twin brother, Asa, and a man Marc had never seen before coming out of the lodge.

"Smile," he whispered in her ear, not letting her go. "This is her week. We shouldn't let what we feel for each other interfere with her happiness."

She looked at him for a moment, anger still lingering in her eyes, but her face relaxed and she smiled brightly at her friend. "That's the only thing you have said so far that's worth listening to."

If he wasn't holding on to her, her smile would have knocked him on his ass. It got him in the gut. He had wondered why it was her his teenage self had gotten it bad for, but now he remembered. It was that slightly lopsided, always-happy smile. On teenage Willa it had been inviting, but on adult Willa… Her whole face lit up and it made him remember that she was one of the few truly beautiful women he had ever met.

"I'm so glad you both made it!" Virginia rushed toward them, grabbing Willa and hugging her tightly. "I've missed you too much, girl."

"I've missed you, too. I'm so happy for you."

"Thank you for coming. I know Costa Rica is a lot to ask."

"You know I wouldn't have missed this," Willa said as Virginia pulled away. "This place is beautiful."

"Wait until you see the rest of it. I freaked out when Carlos brought me here the first time. I thought the man had gone crazy and was asking me to camp in the rain forest."

"I know you too well, baby," the man Marc had never met said as he grinned down at her. "No electricity. No Virginia."

"Damn right." She grinned back at him. "And you, Marc." She hugged him. "You get better-looking every time I see you. How has life in DC been treating you since I saw you last year?"

"It's been all right." He let her go and studied her. Virginia had been a lot like Willa growing up. Quiet. Driven. Too smart for her own good. But unlike Willa, Virginia had always been very artistic. A painter turned interior designer. "Love looks good on you."

"Thanks." She beamed and she grabbed her fiancé's hand. "I want you to meet Carlos. I've decorated his house multiple times. It took me a year. I thought he hated my taste."

"No." Carlos wrapped his arm around her and kissed her cheek. "I just didn't want you to walk out of my life."

"You could have just asked me stay," she said, laughing.

"I had to make you fall in love with me first."

"You're right." She looked back to Willa, still grinning. "Isn't he smooth?"

"It's nice to meet you, Carlos." She shook his hand. "I never thought that when Virginia took the job decorating your house that you would become the love of her life."

"I'm a lucky man. And it's very nice to meet you both." He had one of those knee-weakening smiles. "I wish we could talk longer, but Virginia and I have to meet the planner at the reception site."

"Count me out," said Asa, Virginia's brother, speaking for the first time. "I've been stuck with these two for way too long. They act so sweet they make my damn stomach hurt. Come get a drink with me, Marcus. I'm glad you're finally here." He reached over and ruffled Willa's hair. "You're looking really good in that dress, Willa." Asa's eyes wandered over Willa's body. Marc knew his friend; they were still close. He could see the interest there, and he didn't like it. "I almost didn't recognize you. Being a writer must agree with you. You still single?"

"You still a big pain in the ass?" She smiled, but he could tell she was slightly embarrassed by Asa's comment.

"Yup." He grinned at her. "Come get a drink with us."

"Rain check? I want to get cleaned up a little after my flight."

"Okay." He nodded. "Dinner then. A few of us are going to eat at the open-air restaurant tonight. You'll come with us."

"Sounds good. I'll meet you there." She hugged Virginia again. "I don't want to keep you. We'll catch up later."

"We will." Virginia and Carlos said their goodbyes, leaving the three of them alone.

"Wait until you see the bar they have by the lagoon."

"Maybe I should take a rain check, too, and meet you at

dinner." He looked at Willa, wanting to get her alone again before it would be too hard. "I should check in with work."

"No. You're coming with me. You work too much." Asa gripped Marc's arm and pulled him away. "See you around, Willa."

She grinned widely and he could see the satisfaction in her face. She obviously wanted no part of being alone with him. "See you later, boys."

She walked away from him again, hips swaying hypnotically, and this time he knew he wasn't the only one watching her go.

Chapter 3

Willa looked at herself one last time before she walked out of her room. She had decided to let her hair loose tonight. Literally. She hadn't done much with it other than tie it back since she worked from home, but tonight she would let her natural curls spring free. She wanted to feel pretty tonight. She had noticed the way Marc's eyes had wandered over her body. She felt them on her as she walked away from him, but she didn't want to look good for him. She wanted to look good for herself. She wasn't that same girl who got her heart broken so easily. She had since gotten her doctorate and written bestsellers. She was supporting herself doing something she was good at, that she loved. She wanted to prove to him that even though he hadn't loved her, she loved herself. She wasn't so insecure anymore.

And she was going to make sure he knew that. So with one more fluff of her curls she slipped her key into her bag and walked out of her room. She shouldn't call it a room; it was more like a bungalow. A small house in the middle of the jungle that was surrounded by vibrant gardens filled with colorful flowers and thick jungle trees. There was just as much outdoor living space as there was inside, a covered porch that held rocking chairs, a hammock and a dining room table. In the distance she could hear running water and the chirping of birds. This was the kind of place she could lose herself in her writing. There was no TV, no distractions, just tranquillity.

She didn't know how the resort did it, made the place feel so private when she knew there had to be at least a hundred people working and staying there. But she could only see one other bungalow next door. The main building and all the other bungalows were hidden by nature. She had never experienced anything like it, and she was infinitely glad that Virginia had decided to get married here, and that she looked so happy and beautiful and loved. Even Marc's presence wouldn't put a damper on this occasion.

She came upon the open-air dining room, which was lit with flickering lights that resembled candles. There were plants everywhere, bright flowers that assaulted her eyes with beauty. She felt more like she was in a tropical garden than in a restaurant, and she had to stop for a moment at the entrance to take it all in.

She could feel the romance here. This felt like a place where people came to fall in love.

"Willa." She heard her name and looked up to see Asa waving her over. She had never seen Asa as anything more than a brother. But she had to admit the paramedic looked incredibly handsome in his gray plaid sport coat and white button-down shirt, which revealed just a little bit of his muscular chest.

"I didn't get to hug you before," he said, pulling her into

a tight embrace. "I'm glad you came. It's been too long since I've seen you."

She had always liked Asa, even though he ran with the cool crowd in high school. She liked to think of him as the man with a thousand girlfriends, because as long as she had known him he had never been single. But he wasn't a womanizer. He was just a man who loved women. And it was easy to see why women loved him.

"I would see you more, but I don't want your girlfriend trying to beat me up."

"No girlfriend." He winked at her.

"Really? You went through the entire state already?"

"Something like that." He flashed her a boyish grin. "You didn't have any trouble finding this place, did you?" he asked as he pulled out the chair next to his, near the head of the table. "I got lost three times trying to get here. Those bungalows look nice, but I'm staying in the lodge on the other side of the resort where they have the regular old-fashioned hotel rooms with the big flat-screen TVs and the nice carpet."

"Nature's not your thing, Asa?"

"No. I like nature just fine. I'm just not crazy about feeling like I'm sleeping in it. I live in Hell's Kitchen. I like to hear garbage trucks and my neighbors fighting. I'm not used to hearing birds cawing and trees blowing in the wind. It's creepy."

"You live in Hell's Kitchen? I thought you were still in Hoboken."

"No, girl. I now work for the city of New York. Can't live in Jersey anymore."

She knew a lot of people in New York, but knowing that she had a true friend living nearby made her happy. "I don't live too far from Hell's Kitchen. There's some great restaurants there."

"I know." He grinned at her. "Now that I'm all settled, I plan to take you to some of them."

"Hey." She felt Marc behind her even before she heard his voice. His heavy, warm hand curved over her shoulder, and a rush of tingles slid down her back. She turned around to look at him, to see why he was touching her, only to have her cheek run into his lips. He kissed her there. Not like an old friend would kiss another, but softly, letting his lips linger a little longer than they should. "You're beautiful tonight, Willa," he said so softly only she could hear him.

She didn't know what to do at first. The urge to close her eyes and wrap his words around her like a blanket took over. His compliment caught her completely off guard. It sounded genuine. It felt genuine, too, because she did feel pretty tonight, but she couldn't trust his words. He had lied to her so many times before. He was trying to charm her. A weaker woman would have let him, but there was no way she could forget what he said.

There's no way in hell I would be with her.
She's too weird.

She may well have been, but she hadn't deserved that. Especially when they had been seeing each other for a year at that point. It had been in secret, though. That should have been her first clue to stay away from him.

"Is it just going to be us tonight?" Marc asked Asa as he looked around the large table and then took the chair directly next to hers.

He moved his chair closer to her, his thigh now pressing against hers, causing her to jump at the contact. But she couldn't move away. Asa was on the other side of her at the head of the table. There was no place else for her to go, and she didn't want to lose her cool in front of him by calling out Marc. Asa hadn't known about their secret relationship either, and she wanted to keep it that way.

"Carlos's family should be here soon. I didn't know what to think when my sister told me she was in love with a pro ball player, but he and his family are cool. And if he hurts her he knows I'm going to come after him with one of his baseball bats."

"So protective." Willa smiled at him, trying to ignore the heat that Marc's leg had produced beside hers. "You're not that same kid who used to put fake spiders in her food."

He smiled fondly and shrugged. "I've never seen anybody so afraid of spiders. You could hear that girl scream all the way to Seaside. But I don't bother her much anymore. I grew up."

"Yeah," Marcus said. "We've all grown up a lot since high school." He placed his hand on her thigh, just above her knee, making it clear that his message was just for her. She tried to ignore his touch, pretend that she hadn't noticed the heat, that slight jolt, that shot between her legs. But she couldn't, and suddenly she wished that her long dress wasn't there serving as a barrier. That his big warm hand was directly on her skin, that his fingers were creeping along the inside of thigh.

It was an insane thought, considering how much she wanted to be away from him. But he had always had that power over her. He always made her want to lose herself with him.

She wanted to think that he made her feel this way because she hadn't had sex in so long. Her last relationship had ended almost two years ago, and any man could have had this effect on her. But handsome, charming Asa was sitting on the other side of her, and she felt nothing more than friendship for him.

"Are your parents here, Asa? I haven't seen them yet," she asked, trying to distract herself from the way Marc's hand felt, still on her leg.

"They'll be here in a few days. Virginia banned my mother from any part of the planning. My mother likes traditional. She wants to see Gin in a big white dress in our hometown church. This is definitely not what she pictured. I wish I could be there to see her face when they pull up to the resort. She's going to have a heart attack."

"I almost did," she said, distracted. Marc's hand was still on her leg; his thigh was still pressed against her. He gave her no space, his touch a constant reminder that they had unfinished business in his eyes. "How is your mother?" she turned to Marc, looking him directly in the eye as she pushed his hand off her leg. He caught her fingers, squeezing them softly as he looked back at her. His eyes were trying to send some unspoken message, but she wasn't in the mood to receive it.

She shook his hand off.

"My mother is doing well. She's still in South Carolina, but she's just outside of Charleston now. She's got a boyfriend. He's a police officer. Nice guy. He treats her well. They were getting serious when I was down there for Thanksgiving. I think there might be another wedding in my future."

"How do you feel about your mom getting married?" she asked, remembering the difficult relationship they had.

He looked at her for a long moment, as if he was carefully weighing his words. "She's been through a lot. I want her to be happy."

Willa believed that. Marc's mother was fifteen when she had him and cast out by her very conservative family. She knew that his mother had been too poor, too young and too alone to give him the same stable upbringing the rest of the group had. He had bounced around a lot when he was younger. But all that changed when he was fourteen years old and his mother sent him to live with his aunt and uncle in Short Hills. She was twenty-nine at the time and decided it was time she better herself. She went on to finish high school and got her degree in accounting. But Marc felt abandoned, and when they had first met he was a very quiet, very angry boy.

She had felt sad for him, then. His mother was something they had talked about a lot. "Are you two closer now?"

He nodded. "It took some time. I knew she loved me. She just needed to grow up, and I had to realize that she did what she thought was best. There is no way I would have gone to Howard and gotten such a good job in DC if she hadn't sent me to live with my uncle and aunt."

"You went to Howard?" She shook her head in confusion. "I thought you were set on going to University of Pittsburgh to play football. They gave you a full ride."

"He never even played ball in college. Our boy has gotten himself in the politics game instead," Asa said. "I thought you knew that."

"No." She shook her head, but she couldn't take her eyes off Marc, and for the first time he wouldn't look her in the eye. Football had been so important to him. His teammates had been so important to him, and in the end he had chosen them over her. She had a hard time believing he never played after high school. "I didn't know any of that."

"Yeah," Asa continued. "He's the guy all the politicians go to when they get caught doing something they're not supposed to be doing. The man could make a serial killer look like a saint. You guys didn't keep in touch after high school at all?"

"Why would we?" She turned away from Marc to look at Asa. "He was your best friend, not mine."

The jab didn't go unnoticed by Asa, who looked from Marc to her in confusion. "You guys look like—like…"

He trailed off as he studied each of them. He wasn't stupid. He could see how close they were sitting. He had noticed the lingering kiss Marc had given her when he arrived. "You two look like you're still close."

"We were close," Marc told him, shaking his head. "She's mad at me."

"Mad at you? Why?"

"I was a straight-up asshole to her when we were in high school."

Willa turned around to look at Marc, surprised he admitted it aloud.

"What?" Asa frowned. "Why were you an asshole to Willa?"

But Marc never had the chance to answer because Carlos's family arrived then.

Asa had his hands all over her.

That thought had kept playing on repeat in Marc's head since he entered the dimly lit dining room that night. The air was slightly perfumed with flowers, and when he saw Willa in his best friend's arms, embracing him like he was her lover instead of her friend, something that felt a little like jealousy crept up into his throat.

To Asa, Willa was fair game. Single, no attachments, successful and looking damn good in the dress she wore tonight. He had never known about their yearlong relationship, that she was his first, that she was the only one he had ever really been in love with. He couldn't blame Asa for wanting her. And he sure as hell couldn't blame himself for doing what he had to do to make sure Asa stayed away. Because in Marc's mind, even though he knew it wasn't true, he felt like Willa was still his girl.

Too bad she hated his guts.

Since Carlos's family had arrived she hadn't spoken

to him unless she absolutely had to. Thinking that if she ignored him he would go away. But he wasn't going anywhere. He was going to be in her face until they had it out about what had happened with them.

Her hand brushed his as she reached for her wineglass and she shot him a look full of heat. He knew he was in her space, knew he was too close. All evening she kept bumping into him, her shoulder, her arm, her leg, and it sent a little jolt through him each time.

That, coupled with the coral dress she wore tonight, made it hard for him to have any clear thoughts. All that bare silky skin of her arms and shoulders. It was distracting. The dress was only held up by one little tie at the back of her neck. All he had to do was pull. One good tug and the dress would tumble down, and if didn't, he would have no problem pulling the rest down and revealing that creamy distracting skin.

Willa's laugh snapped him out those thoughts, but as he looked at her with her head thrown back and her throat exposed, new thoughts popped into his head. Thoughts of him running his lips down the seam her neck, thoughts of his body over her nude one, thoughts of her curls spread over his pillow and a look of pleasure on her face.

He had it bad.

Nobody affected him like this. No woman. Not even the one he had thought he was going to marry.

"You guys are crazy," she said, still laughing. "This was fun, but you wore me out. I think I'm going to head back to my room and relax."

"We'll see you at breakfast tomorrow?" Julia, Carlos's older sister, asked. "The lovebirds are going to take a break from planning to grace us with their presence tomorrow morning."

"That sounds nice," she said. "I'll be there."

"Meet us at the Cala Lagoon at nine. Rumor is that there's going to be crepes."

"You know I won't miss crepes." She stood up. "Good night. I'll see you all in the morning."

"I'll walk you back." Marc stood. He knew that this was the chance he needed to get her alone, to apologize. He knew the longer he waited, the harder it would be to get her off his mind. She had already spent too much time there as it was.

"You don't have to." Her smile dropped as she turned to look at him. "I'm a big girl. I think I can make it back just fine by myself."

"I insist. It's dark."

"The resort is well lit." Her eyes sparked. He saw resistance there and stubbornness and heat. He kind of liked it. "I appreciate your offer, but it's *not* necessary."

"It *is* necessary. I won't be able to sleep tonight unless I know you're safe in your room. Just let me be a gentleman and do this."

"Gentleman? Ha! I think it's going to take a little more than a walk back to my room for me to think of you as a gentleman."

"I'm not doing this for you. I'm doing this for myself." He wasn't going to quit. Didn't she know that? Willa had always been willful, but didn't she understand it would be better for both of them if she just let him have his say?

"You don't have to worry. I'll text you when I get there."

"But you don't have my number."

"Let's keep it that way. See ya."

"Well, damn," they heard Asa say.

They both turned to look at him and noticed the table around them had gone silent. Every pair of eyes had turned to them, surely wondering what the hell was going on. Her smile reappeared, but her eyes didn't lose that annoyed spark. "I'm kidding. Walk me back."

She stepped away from the table, her body stiff, but her hips still swaying that seductive sway. "Stop staring at my ass," she added when they were out of earshot.

"I can't help it. It grew."

Her head snapped around. She scowled at him, but he couldn't help but grin at her.

"I like your big ass, Willa. I like it very much."

Her eyes narrowed and her lips twisted, like she was trying to prevent a smile, but she failed and that lopsided grin of hers appeared. "Thank you. I'm quite proud of it," she said, walking once again.

"You really do look good, Wil. I mean it. I can't stop looking at you."

"You're surprised the ugly duckling turned into a pretty good-looking chick?"

"You're not pretty good-looking, you're beautiful."

"I would say thank you, but I won't. I'm not sure I can believe you, judging from our past and your present role of helping slimy politicians become more slimy."

"You don't have to believe me," he said as they left the dining room completely and walked onto the candlelit path that led back to the villas. "I wouldn't lie to you about that." He shook his head. "You're incredible." He moved ahead so that he was beside her instead of behind her. He needed to see her face as they talked. Her words might be biting, but her face always gave everything away.

"I didn't want to cause a scene before, but you really can stop following me back to my bungalow. I'll be fine. It's just beyond this bend."

"You know I'm not here just because I want to see you back to your room. I want to talk to you."

"I really don't want to listen to you, but since you won't leave, talk."

"How could you think I would forget you? I spent every free moment with you. You were important to me."

"Whatever, Marc. I'm over it. So what, you told your friends I was like your 'practice dummy' when they found us kissing? So what if you denied our yearlong relationship to your teammates? It doesn't matter that you told them that you would never be with someone like me. I grew up. I grew a backbone. You actually did me a favor, because now I know I'll never be with another guy who doesn't think I'm worthy of him."

"You're right. You never should be with a guy like that, with an idiot like I was. But I think you got your revenge when you killed me off in your second novel. I thought the decapitation was a bit much, but it was so well done, even I have to admit I had it coming."

"You knew that was you?" They came to the steps of her bungalow and she stopped. She couldn't hide the surprise on her face.

"Former jock who humiliated his killer in high school? Who else could it have been? My only question is, do you kill off everybody that's ever hurt you in your books, or am I the only one with that honor?"

"Just you." She searched his face as if she were trying to see if he was telling the truth. "You read my book?"

"I read all four of your books. The last one was my favorite. I didn't know you were so dark or so damn funny. One moment I'm so wrapped up in your words, racking my mind trying to figure out where you were going, the next minute I'm laughing so hard there are tears streaming down my face. I'm telling you the truth when I say you're incredible. I am amazed by you."

"Thank you," she said softly as she walked up the steps

to her door and he followed, not wanting to let her go just yet. "I appreciate that."

"I'm sorry, you know. I'll always be sorry for what I did to you. I hated myself for it. I hated myself because I did to you what I thought my mother did to me. I threw you away. I was a coward. I thought I needed those guys. I thought I needed their respect and acceptance to feel worthy, but I didn't. I lost my best friend when I said those words that day, and you don't know how sorry I am for it."

Her eyes filled with tears. He hadn't expected that. Her anger, yes. That he deserved in droves. But seeing that he had hurt her so much was painful. "You said you loved me. How could you have lied to me like that?"

He closed the distance between them and wrapped his arms around her, bringing her close enough that his lips touched her skin. She didn't fight this time, just let him hold her. Let his lips graze her forehead.

"Damn it, Willa. I didn't lie to you. I never lied to you. I loved you. I know I did wrong by denying us, but I loved you. I couldn't have spent a year with you if I didn't."

"I believed what you said to your teammates that day. That you were only with me to practice your game. I used to wonder how we happened. You were the goddamn quarterback and I was the nerd. We couldn't have been more clichéd if we tried."

"I was a defensive end," he corrected her as he dropped a soft kiss on her forehead. "I liked you because you made me laugh and I thought you were cute." He kissed the bridge of her nose, causing her to shut her eyes. "I was with you because I was amazed by how smart you were. You were almost too smart for me. I felt dumb around you sometimes. But I forgave you for it because you were a damn good kisser."

She opened those big pretty eyes of hers and stared up

at him, but instead of tears in her eyes he saw curiosity mixed with a little bit of hunger. Or maybe he was seeing his eyes mirrored in her own. She was fully pressed against him from her breasts to her toes. All of her softness, all of her warmth, was seeping into him. He felt kind of drunk, kind of heady, like a boy with his first love instead of a man who had had more than his fair share of women. But that's what she did to him. She made him feel like no one else ever had, and now that he felt her against him again, he was sure that no other woman could ever make him feel this way.

"I was a good kisser?" she asked with a slight hitch in her breath. "I *was* a champ, wasn't I?" She grinned at him and it hit him right in his chest. He had never seen a smile as sexy as hers. "Taught you everything you know, didn't I?"

"You sure did." He grinned back at her, glad to see her smiling at him.

"I didn't know anything, Marc. Nothing. You were my first everything."

Chapter 4

"You weren't my first kiss," he said to her as she watched his mouth grow closer to her once again. "But you were my first and greatest everything else." His lips dropped to her neck, kissing her in that little curve that always felt so good to be kissed. Especially by him. His lips were full and warm, and the way they expertly trailed up her neck made her wish that it wasn't just her neck that he was kissing.

Her eyes drifted shut as his hands slid over her hips on top of the soft material of her dress, which had suddenly become confining. She wanted to feel his skin against hers, his hard body on top of hers. She may have been his first, they both might have been young and inexperienced then, but he always took his time with her, went slow, made sure she was comfortable, made sure she always felt good in the end. She had thought sex would get better as she got older, but it hadn't. She hadn't wanted to admit it, but she had foolishly compared every other man she had been with to him.

And now he was here again, touching her slowly, kissing her in a way only he could, and it was driving her crazy.

"What are you doing to me?" she asked breathlessly.

"Hell, I wish I knew." She knew he was going to take her mouth; she anticipated the feel of his lips on hers. She wanted to taste him, to savor him, to take this new memory of him and lock it up.

"I've missed you," he whispered right as his mouth touched hers, and that snapped her right out of her lust-filled fog. She was going to let the boy who broke her heart suck her in again.

She shoved him away. "No. Bad. Just no."

"Willa," he groaned.

"Don't you 'Willa' me. What are you doing with your hands all over me? And where do you get off telling me you miss me? You don't miss me! You've probably got a whole other squad of football players waiting somewhere so you can humiliate—"

"Willa, enough!" he barked, and she jumped. "I'm sorry." He cupped her face and rested his forehead against hers. "You know I'm sorry. I hurt you and I have been feeling like shit about it since you walked out of my life." He lifted his head and looked into her eyes. "You don't have to forgive me, but the least you can do is believe me when I tell you that."

She closed her eyes briefly, because his gaze was too much for her. He wasn't lying to her. It would be easier if he were. "I do believe you. I just don't think I'm ready to stop being mad at you yet."

"Okay. Fair enough." He nodded and stepped away from her. "Good night."

She watched him walk away from her, expecting him to say more, but he didn't. He didn't even look back at her.

She knew that preventing him from really kissing her was the right thing to do. She didn't need him to invade her thoughts any more than he already had, but she kind of wished she hadn't stopped him. She kind of wished she had been swept away by his kiss, by one of those mind-numbing kisses that made all coherent thoughts flee. It would have been nice to go to bed still feeling the warmth from his mouth, instead of this emptiness in her chest.

"Hey, Willa," he called. She looked over to see him on the steps of the bungalow next to hers. It took her a moment to process what he was doing there, but when she saw him take the key out of his pocket and place it in the door she knew there was no escaping him this trip.

"Let's head over to breakfast tomorrow together. And don't think of going without me. I get up early."

Marc was serious about being an early riser. When Willa walked outside to her outdoor living room, she saw him in his. His eyes were closed, his arms were stretched high above his head, and he was shirtless. She had known he was in good shape before. She had seen the way his clothing fit, she had felt his hard, hot body pressed against hers the day before, but seeing him...

Her mouth went dry. She didn't need to be close to see how ripped his body was. All those muscles covered by that rich dark skin. She had never been a sucker for built men—guys with muscles were never her thing—but Marcus was impressive. And the urge to walk across the little path that separated their bungalows and inspect him more closely was overwhelming.

He opened his eyes then and looked directly at her.

She had been caught ogling him red-handed, and all she could think to say was "Hi."

"Hi." He gave her a knowing smile. "I was just doing my post-workout stretches."

"Um, you're good at them."

"Come over here and I'll show you how they're done."

"That's okay," she said quickly. "I have to go get dressed."

"Maybe later?" His grin grew a little wider, and if possible, sexier. "I'll meet you at your place in an hour. I know where we are meeting for breakfast."

He was there exactly an hour later. Today he was in more relaxed clothing than she was used to seeing him in—an aqua-colored polo and some well-fitting shorts. He wore a smile, too, like he knew something that she didn't. She wanted to knock it off his face, but she found it too damn appealing.

"I like your hair like this, Wil." He lifted his hand to touch her curls. She would have been fine if that was where he'd stopped, but somehow his hand slid down to cup her chin, and his thumb was suddenly stroking her jawline. "It's pretty."

His touch felt nice, not sexual, not hot like his other touches had, just nice. Her eyes started to drift shut again as his touch began to hypnotize her, but she forced them open, refusing to be taken in by him.

She slapped his hand away. "I accepted your apology. So you can quit whatever it is you're up to."

"I'm not up to anything."

"Really? How did your bungalow get next to mine?"

"I assure you I wasn't here when they built it. I think whoever designed this resort decided to put that one next to this one."

"You know what I mean."

"No, I don't, Dr. Arthur. You know I'm a slow Southern boy. You might have to break it down for me."

"Did you ask them to put you in the bungalow next to mine?"

"That seems a little stalker-ish."

"It is!"

"What if I did? What would you think about that?"

"That you were a psycho planning to make a skin suit out of me."

He raised his hands in defense. "Hold on there, Miss Imagination. I think writing those novels has made you paranoid."

"It really has," she admitted. "Sometimes I sleep with the lights and TV on. Even last night I was kind of scared."

"Were you?"

"Yes. Even though I know nothing is going to happen to me, I still find myself afraid to sleep alone in a new place."

He put his hand on her shoulder and squeezed. "I can come over tonight if you want."

"I'd rather be turned into a skin suit."

"Ouch, girl." He touched his chest. "That one hit me right here."

"Pity. I was hoping it hit you lower."

He laughed, the same rich deep laugh he had when she first knew him. It made her warm all over then, and it still had the same effect on her now.

"I think I'm going to have to start wearing a cup around you."

"It's not a bad idea, especially since you insist on forcing your presence on me."

"I'm not forcing my presence on you." He looped his arm around her shoulder and brought her close to him, dropping a kiss on her forehead. "We're just old friends who need to get to know each other again."

She leaned into him. "I have a feeling you would like to get to know me again without my clothes on."

He shook his head. "I have nothing to say to that."

"Nothing to say to that?" She looked up at him. "You do want to see me naked, don't you?"

He laughed again. "Come on, Willa. Let's get some breakfast."

"Look up there!" Marc pointed to the thick trees above them as they walked the path to breakfast.

"What?" She inched closer to him. It wasn't the first time he had alerted her to something he saw on their walk. The first time was a small green reptile, the second it was one of the biggest bugs she had ever seen. She was just hoping he wasn't pointing out something bigger than that.

"Toucan."

She followed his finger to see that there was a beautiful bird with a colorful beak sitting on a branch above them. "He's gorgeous," she said, sighing.

"Why do you sound relieved?"

"I lived in New York for ten years. The only wildlife I see are pigeons and the occasional rat in the subway. I just wasn't sure what to expect."

"A snake maybe?"

She nodded. "I love trees and plants and fresh tropical air. But after seeing that bug I'm not sure I like all the creepy-crawly things that come along with plants and trees and fresh tropical air."

"That's too bad, because there's a little snake right there just off the path."

"What?" She grabbed on to him, holding him tightly around the middle.

"There's a little snake right over there. Really colorful, probably poisonous."

"That's not funny, Marc!" She buried her face in his

chest, not sure if he was telling the truth, but too creeped out to look and find out.

"I'm not laughing, Willa," he said as he wrapped his arms around her. "I read that a lot of snakes give dry bites, meaning no venom comes out. Even if the venom did come out, only one percent of people die from snakebites. And we're at this resort. I'm sure if you got bit there is some antivenin somewhere around here."

"I hate you so much right now."

"I can live with that. Come on. Let's keep walking. We're almost there. I won't let the little guy get you."

"What are you going to do? Break him in half?"

"Didn't you know I was a snake charmer? I work with much bigger serpents than him in Washington."

"That's right. You clean up their messes."

"I wouldn't call it that. I give them the opportunity to make better choices."

"That's a nice way of putting it. Do you like your job?"

"Hate it," he said as they walked on.

"Really?"

"I'm an extremely well-paid babysitter. I've seen kinder-gartners who were more qualified to hold public office."

"I always thought you were going to be a teacher. I saw you with those kids when you were a camp counselor. You were so good with them. You've never considered work-ing with kids?"

"I thought about it, but being a teacher didn't fit in with the lifestyle I wanted to have. Until I moved in with my aunt and uncle, I was piss-poor. They showed me that a better life was attainable, and I wanted to show them that I could do well for myself."

"I'm sure they would have been just as proud of you if you had become a teacher."

"Maybe, but honestly I didn't do it just for that. DC is

exciting at first, and I had all these powerful people listening to me, asking me what I thought, coming to me for help. Plus it was a job I could use my mind with. For a long time the only way I thought I could become successful was playing pro ball. I think I wanted to prove to myself that I had more to offer. Besides, this job makes my mama real proud, and she brags to all her friends that I know the president."

"Do you?"

"We've met. He told me he hopes he never has to see me again, because that means something has gone terribly wrong in his life."

His words made Willa laugh, and she almost forgot that she still had her arm wrapped around him, that there was no space between their sides as they walked. That his hard, warm body felt good against hers, and that in this unfamiliar landscape she felt safe with him. But she remembered as soon as they came to the opening and saw Virginia and her soon-to-be husband sitting at a table in front of the small man-made lagoon.

She couldn't miss the curious look in her friend's eyes as she spotted them together. But there was no judgment there. Only curiosity.

"Good morning!" Willa greeted them as she distanced herself from Marc. "How did the planning go last night?"

"I'm sure Carlos is bored to death with it." Virginia looped her arm through Willa's. "He said he wanted to help plan, but I think he's had enough of me going on about the details."

"No, baby. I really don't mind. Your freaky attention to detail is one of the many reasons I fell in love with you."

"Charmer." She grinned adoringly at him. "You don't have to try so hard." She dropped her voice to a whisper. "You're going to get lucky tonight anyway. I'm going to take a little walk with Willa while we wait for everyone else to get here. You talk to Marc. He's a man and likes sports and stuff."

She led Willa down the path that wound around the lagoon. There was a small waterfall gently flowing into a pool. "How did you choose this place, Gin? It's so beautiful."

"I didn't. Carlos's family is from Costa Rica. He brought me here when I came to meet his grandmother. We only came for a few days, but it was an amazing three days. I knew we had to get married here. Now enough about me. What's going on with you and Marc?"

"What?" She laughed uneasily. "There's nothing going on. I haven't seen him since we graduated."

"Really? You two looked kind of cozy when you walked in."

"That was nothing. He just happens to be staying next door to me. We walked over together."

"Oh? I also heard that you were sitting kind of close together at dinner last night. That's kind of odd for somebody you haven't seen since high school."

"Who told you that? They were exaggerating."

"Marcus Simpson has grown into one fine-looking man, Wil. When's the last time you had sex?"

"That's none of your business!"

"Since when? And it's been that long, huh? It wouldn't be so bad if you had a little thing going on. You know I wouldn't judge."

"Why are you so interested in us all of a sudden?"

"It's not so sudden," she admitted. "When I called him to invite him to the wedding, the first thing he asked about was you. He has always asked about you. Why didn't you two keep in touch?"

She shrugged. "Asa asked me that. I guess we had nothing to say."

Virginia looked disappointed. "I thought you two had a crush on each other in high school. I always wanted you two to get together."

"You did?"

"I know it was silly. But it would be nice to have my best friends get together."

"Gin," Carlos called to her. "Everybody is here. Let's eat."

All the wedding guests were supposed to meet back at the main lodge a few hours later. They were heading out for a "jungle excursion," as Virginia called it. Marc didn't know what exactly to expect. He only wished he was walking over with Willa and not by himself. Her curvy little body felt good tucked into his, but he knew he needed to put some space between them. He hadn't missed the look Virginia gave them when they walked into breakfast that morning with their arms wrapped around each other. There nothing going on between them except an attraction that hadn't died. He knew she felt it, too. Every look, every smile, every unintentional touch told him so. But there was no need to stir up rumors with their friends if nothing was going on between them.

He walked inside the lodge to find that most of their party was already there. Virginia and Carlos were talking with who he thought might be their tour guide. All three of them were wearing sturdy hiking boots. Asa was wearing sneakers, shorts and a long-sleeved FDNY T-shirt. Whatever they had planned for the day it seemed they were all prepared to be active. He was glad he had changed into his workout clothes.

Asa came over to him. "You ready for this?" He brought

his knee up to his chest, stretching just like he did before track practice. "I've read some crazy shit about this rain forest tour. Virginia didn't even pick the easy one. She picked the zip-line canopy tour with a visit to the open-air serpentarium."

"What the hell is a serpentarium?"

"It's where they keep all the snakes and reptiles. The place is fenced in, but they don't keep the snakes in cages. They live in trees."

"Oh."

"I'm surprised at my sister, but this year she has become a bit of an adrenaline junkie. She's gone skydiving and bungee jumping. She's even done a couple of mud races with me. I can't blame Carlos, either. Even he thinks she's a little crazy."

His thoughts immediately went to Willa, who lived in New York City and thought taking the subway was enough adventure for her. She couldn't even look at the tiny snake he saw this morning. He wondered if she knew what she was in for.

And then she walked in wearing a cute little sundress with tiny flowers on it. On her feet were gold sandals, and her hair was pulled back in a tight bun. Everyone looked at her.

"I can see I'm not dressed properly for this rain forest excursion."

"That's okay, Wil," Virginia said. "I wasn't really clear about what we were doing today. I wanted you guys to be surprised. You can go back and change. We'll wait for you."

"What exactly do you have in store for us? I don't think I was prepared for more than a tour of the resort."

"I'm not feeling too good," Marc spoke up and stepped

forward and took her hand. "Willa and are going to sit this tour out. Take a lot of pictures."

He took her out of the lodge before anyone could say anything else.

"Why did you pull me out of there? What makes you think I want to spend the afternoon with you?"

"Fine. Go back in there. I'm sure you'll have lots of fun on the zip-line tour, and the trip to the serpentarium would have been the thrill of your life."

"A serpentarium?" Her face fell. "Is that like the reptile house at the Bronx Zoo?"

"Kind of. Only there's no thick glass between you and the wildlife."

She shivered. "What the hell is wrong with Virginia? That's nobody's idea of a good time."

"It's hers, and you would have gone along and pretended you weren't scared shitless because you wouldn't have wanted to disappoint your friend."

She nodded. "I'm kind of scared of heights, too. I really thought I was going to spend this entire trip in my bathing suit with a drink in my hand. I even put on my bathing suit before I left my bungalow."

"That can be accomplished," he said. "Let's go swimming. I know just the place."

They headed to a freshwater swimming pool on the edge of the resort. Surrounded by lush trees and decorated with a waterfall, it looked like nature had put the pool there instead of the resort. The pool was nearly empty; only one other couple were there, and they were sunbathing on the sunny side of it.

"How did you know this was here?" Willa asked as she looked around in awe. The entire resort felt secluded, but this pool defined paradise. The clear rippling water almost looked too perfect to swim in, and he watched Willa stare at it as if she were mesmerized.

"I asked the front desk where I could find a pool with no kids. This one is supposed to be adults only."

"Oh." She looked away from the pool to him. "I should thank you."

"For what?"

"Saving me from the serpentarium. You sacrificed your afternoon for me."

"It's nothing. I'll go get some towels. Get in."

She shook her head. "I'll wait for you."

Something had shifted between them in that moment. She had accepted his apology before, but right now he felt completely forgiven. "Okay. Pick some good chairs for us. I'll be right back."

He turned away to get them each a plush towel, but when he turned back he froze, too caught up in watching Willa strip off her dress to move. She wore white. A white one-piece suit with cutouts on each side, baring her small waist. It was held together by two intersecting gold rings at her hips.

His groin tightened painfully.

"You're staring." She looked up at him.

"Yeah. Sorry." His mouth was too dry to speak any more. Willa looked good every time he saw her, but in his wildest dreams he never thought she could look so tempting wearing pure white.

She turned around, revealing her beautiful backside to him. "Is it too much?" She smoothed her hands over her bottom self-consciously. "I saw it online and thought what the hell, but now that I'm wearing it I feel silly."

"Silly?"

She nodded. "Like a girl like me shouldn't wear a suit like this."

"What kind of bathing suit do you think you should wear? A scuba suit? Don't be one of those women who can't see how sexy she is."

She blinked at him for a moment, her expression going thoughtful. "I wish I knew what to say to that."

"Don't say anything. Get in the pool."

She did as he said, walking away from him again and slowly slipping into the pool. He was glad she walked away from him, not only because he got a glimpse of her outstanding behind, but because he desperately needed some space between them. Looking at her was sensory overload. It was all curves and skin. The contrast of her white bathing suit against all that pretty brown skin. Being near her without touching her was painful. It was taking everything in his power not to peel that little strip of fabric off of her and get to know her body all over again.

"It's perfect." She looked back at him, her hands on her hips as she stood knee-deep in the water. "Why are your pants still on? Take them off."

He look at her for a long moment, not sure if she understood what effect her words had on him. His swim shorts were baggy, but he wasn't sure they could cover his burgeoning arousal.

"I'll be there in a minute." He turned his back to her. Taking a few deep breaths, he slipped off his shorts and T-shirt.

She was fully submerged when he turned back, just her head sticking out of the water, but her eyes were on him, studying him, taking him in. He stepped into the pool, and she was right. The water was perfect, warm enough to feel comfortable, but cool enough to be refreshing.

"I really feel like I'm swimming in the middle of a rain forest," she said to him as he made his way to her.

"That's because you are, Willa."

She smiled softly. "I guess I am. I meant that I don't feel like I'm in the middle of a resort here. It just feels like it's you and me and no one else around for miles."

He knew what she meant. He glanced around him to see the plants and trees, the waterfall flowing behind her, the sounds of birds in the distance. It was just him and her in the water. He thought he had romance before with other women, candlelit dinners and time spent in hot tubs, but he had never felt like this with any of them.

"Does it make you nervous?"

"What?" Her eyes grew wide.

"Being alone with me when everybody else is zip-lining through the jungle as we speak."

"No." She shook her head, standing up so she could walk deeper into the water. "I am feeling a little disappointed, though."

"Disappointed?" he asked, feeling a little blow to his ego.

"Yeah. I was really hoping you had on a Speedo under those shorts." She stopped at the edge of the pool just before the waterfall. Only her head was sticking out of the water, but the water was so clear he could still see every inch of her body. She must have known he was staring, because she inched closer to him, grinning with a satisfied smile. "I've got a thing for thighs, and judging by how hard your chest is, I was imagining that your thighs were pretty spectacular."

"You flirting with me, Dr. Arthur?"

"No." She shook her head firmly. "I would never. I'm an honest person and I felt the need to tell you that I honestly think you have a superb-looking body." She reached for him, sliding her fingers up his arms. "You also have a superb-feeling body." She surprised him by wrapping her arms around him and resting her chin on his shoulder.

Her entire body was pressed against him, but it wasn't enough. He skimmed his hands down the back of her thighs before he gripped them and slid them around his waist. "Damn it, Willa." He grew rock hard then. With her wrapped around him all he could think of was how easy it would be to slip her bathing suit over and slide inside her.

She leaned back a little, looking into his eyes. She studied him again for a moment before she cupped his cheek in her hand. "What would your girlfriend say if she saw us like this right now?"

"What girlfriend?" He frowned at her. "I haven't been with anybody for the last nine months."

"Why not?"

"I was engaged."

"What happened?"

"She was smart and beautiful and ruthless."

"She was a lawyer?"

"Yes." He laughed. "She was the perfect wife for a Washington insider. She just wasn't the perfect wife for me."

"You broke it off?"

"No. She did. I thank God for that. I probably would have gone through with it. When I gave her that ring I made a promise to her. I had told myself I would never break another promise to a woman again."

"You broke a lot of promises to women before?"

"No." He shook his head. "Just to you. I promised you I would always be there for you, and when it counted the most, I failed you."

She looked at him with slight surprise. "You really are sorry, aren't you?"

"I wouldn't have apologized if I wasn't."

She kissed his cheek, letting her lips linger there for a long moment. He closed his eyes, content to have this warm girl wrapped around him in this warm pool in the middle of paradise.

He stroked his fingers over the cutouts in her suit, the feel of her smooth, wet skin more erotic to him than anything else. "What would you have said if I told you I did have a girlfriend?"

"I wouldn't have said anything to you. But I would have had to explain to the police why I tried to drown you."

He laughed, his whole body shaking, causing it to rub against hers. He could feel her nipples scraping his chest through her suit.

She hugged him tightly, rubbing her lips along his jaw before kissing him there. Her kisses were sweet, almost innocent. He felt like he did when they were together, when he was seventeen and unsure if anybody had really loved him except for her.

"You want me, Marc?"

"What kind of question is that?" He cupped her bottom, moving her against him. "We both feel that."

A splash on the other side of the pool alerted him to the fact that they weren't alone, that they weren't miles away from the world, that they weren't in a little magical bubble where coherent thoughts ceased to exist.

They both turned their heads to see the source of the splash and saw a woman emerge from the water.

"Oh my God!" Willa whispered. "Is she naked?"

"Yeah, and it would appear that her man is, too." Willa's head swiveled to see a man with white hair and a bit of a belly kick his swim trunks to the side and step into the pool.

She turned back to him. "Did you know this pool was clothing optional?"

"No. I didn't think adult-only meant clothing optional."

She turned away from him again. "Those things look

like giant navel oranges. They're too round. They have to be fake, right?"

"I'm not looking at her."

"Why not? You have to see those things."

"I'm looking at you, and you look a hell of a lot better than a woman who can be compared to produce."

"My goodness, Marc." She rested her forehead against his. "I've spent so long being mad at you that I forgot why I fell in love with you in the first place."

Her words caused his body to go on full alert. Was it possible for them to fall in love again? He knew it was for him, because a big part of him had never stopped loving her.

"Tag! You're it!" The naked couple on the other side of the pool were chasing each other, not really bothering them, but breaking the bubble around them once again.

"You remember how to play air hockey?" she asked him.

"Yes. I remember that you made it your life's work to never let me win a game."

"You let me win. You think I didn't know that?"

"Sometimes," he admitted. "I liked to see you happy."

"Well, you can see me happy again." She swam away from him. "There's a rec room in the main lodge. I challenge you. Best out of five. Winner buys the drinks tonight."

He swam after her, catching up to her as she stepped out of the pool, her beautiful behind wiggling in his face.

"Are you hungry?" he asked her. He knew he was, and it wasn't for food. "There's a little café here if you want to grab a quick bite. Dinner is not until eight tonight."

"Sounds good," she said, toweling herself off. "Do you think they have cake here?" she asked him as she dragged the towel across her hips. "I could really go for something sweet."

"Yeah," he said distractedly. "I could, too. There's just one thing I have to do first."

"What?"

He grabbed the edges of her towel and tugged on them until her body was pressed against his again. She looked up at him, curiosity in her eyes, but that changed when he inched his mouth closer to hers. He didn't want to steal a kiss, he didn't want to take her by surprise, he wanted her to know it was coming. He wanted her to be an active participant instead of a bystander.

She leaned in, meeting his lips with her own. She was the first one to kiss—a soft, sweet full-lipped peck, like the ones she use to give him when they were teenagers. But they weren't teenagers anymore, and she looked him in the eyes and slid her hands up his neck, stroking her thumbs over his cords.

"Kiss me again, Marc." He obeyed her order, taking her mouth immediately. She opened for him, setting the pace, returning his kiss slowly and deeply. Her mouth was familiar, her lips were warm and soft, and if he had to pick a place to spend the rest of his life he would spend it right there with her, kissing him like this.

He broke that kiss, but he didn't have his fill of her lips yet. He liked those soft, sweet pecks she gave him best of all, and so he kissed her mouth half a dozen times until she was sighing and giggling like the girl he had once known.

"I was right," he said when he finally pulled away.

"About what?"

"You. You're one hell of a kisser."

Chapter 5

A little van had picked them up to take them to dinner that night. It was a surprise to them all, because Virginia and Carlos had been so secretive about the events they had planned for the week. But Willa had been delighted when the van pulled right onto the sand and she saw that a three-piece band was playing and that colorful lanterns lit up the beach.

Delighted was the only way she could describe the way she was feeling. She'd had a good day, the best day she'd had in years. They didn't do any of the exciting things everybody else did. There was no adrenaline rush that came with soaring over the forest, no thrill of seeing snakes in the wild. They went swimming, and played air hockey and Ping-Pong. They ate thick sandwiches and drank juice made with fresh fruit. They had kissed sweetly by the pool with a waterfall serving as a backdrop. They had laughed. They were comfortable. They had a good day.

She was feeling relaxed and kind of giddy as she stepped out of the van and onto the cool, wet sand. As she slipped off her sandals she heard Marc's deep voice behind her, animatedly talking about something with Asa. She forced herself not to look behind her at him, even though she was very tempted to see again how good he looked tonight in his light-colored suit with no tie. But she didn't. She felt like she was a girl again, like it was after the first time he had kissed her and she was trying to hide how much she was falling for him.

Things were different now, of course. She was a grown woman with open eyes who knew that it was just the beautiful setting and the nostalgia of being around somebody that she once loved. She knew this feeling would fade when she returned to New York, returned to normal life. But for now she was going to enjoy herself.

"Willa, my love!" Virginia's mother greeted her. She must have arrived with the bride and groom and his parents, because she hadn't been with them in the van. "It's so good to see you." She hugged her. "How have you've been?"

"I have been wonderful. How about yourself?"

"I have to admit I was terrified of the kind of wedding this was going to be, but now that I'm here, I see it's going to be beautiful. I should just trust that my daughter has impeccable taste."

"She does, and with men, too. Carlos seems very sweet."

"He is." She nodded. "He's had a bit of a reputation as a lady-killer, but he is clearly in love with her and that's all I could ask for." She looked over to her daughter, who was deep in conversation with her future husband and smiling as if no one else were around.

"I'm happy for her," Willa said truthfully.

"Me, too. And I must say you look amazing. I know

your parents weren't thrilled when you quit your job, but I was glad when you did. I'm so glad you followed your dreams."

"Thank you. I'm glad I did, too."

"Hey, Mama Bear." Asa strolled over with Marc at his side. "Did you settle in okay?" He wrapped his arm around his mother and kissed her forehead.

"We did. Thank you. Your sister reserved a deluxe bungalow for us. I've never seen anything like it."

"Hello, Dr. Andersen." Marc reached out to hug the woman. "You look beautiful tonight."

"Thank you, sir. I heard from your uncle that they moved you up to vice president of your firm. That man is so proud of you I think he could bust. Your aunt and uncle couldn't have any children, but I don't think you realized how much of a blessing you were when you came into their life. They love you as much as they would have loved their own child."

"Thank you, Dr. Andersen. I appreciate that."

"Don't thank me. It's the truth."

A waiter carrying glasses of champagne approached them. Asa grabbed a glass for his mother and Marc grabbed a glass for Willa and then wrapped his arm around her, smoothing his hand down her arm. Asa and his mother looked at them, but Marc didn't seem to notice.

"Are you cold?" he asked her, rubbing his hand down her again. "I'll give up my jacket."

"You don't have to. I'm fine now." She had been a little chilled with the ocean breeze blowing, but she was too busy enjoying the scenery around her to mind. Now she was enjoying his hand stroking down her arm.

"You've got goose bumps."

"You have that effect on me."

He grinned at her, shaking his head in disbelief. "I'm not sure if it's a good thing or a bad thing."

"What is this?" Asa asked, pointing at them. "What's going on between you two?"

"Why are you asking?" Willa stepped a little closer to Marc, wrapping her arm around Marc. "Because he was gentleman enough to see that I was cold and offer me his coat. You could have done the same and I would be cuddled with you instead of him."

"Really?"

"I've got a free side. Why don't you come over here and find out for yourself?"

"My favorite people!" Virginia walked over. "How are you feeling, Marc? We missed you guys this afternoon." She looked at them the same way her brother had, and Willa was tempted to move away from Marc, but she didn't want to.

"I'm feeling much better. How was zip-lining?"

"Exhilarating."

"And the snakes?"

"Amazing. I held a boa constrictor." Virginia smirked at them. "I'm more interested in how you guys spent your afternoon."

"Yeah, Gin," Asa said. "I was just going to ask the same thing."

"We checked out the pool and played air hockey," Willa informed them. "Then we had lunch and took a nap in our separate rooms." And that was the truth. They didn't need to know about the heart-melting kisses that had stayed with her all day.

"Oh, leave them alone, you two," Dr. Andersen scolded her children. "They are just old friends."

"Thank you," Marc said. "We are friends."

"You're welcome, honey. Now if you all will excuse me, I need to see what my husband is up to."

She walked away, and Marc's lips drifted to Willa's neck. "Okay, baby." He kissed her there. "Now that Dr. Andersen is gone, tell them how we really spent our afternoon." He kissed her neck again before moving to her throat, and if she weren't surrounded by people, she would have shut her eyes and enjoyed his mouth. "Don't leave out any details."

"Marc!" She hit him in the stomach. "Quit it!"

He lifted his head, chuckling. "Willa told you guys the truth. That's how we spent the afternoon."

"I'm afraid of snakes and heights, Gin. Marc sacrificed himself to stay with me."

"I get the snake thing, but heights? I didn't know that. I would have never planned zip-lining if I had."

"I know, but I want you to do whatever it is you want during this week, not worry about me."

"You didn't know Wil was afraid of heights?" Marc looked down at Willa. "She always has been. Remember that time she nearly freaked out when the Ferris wheel got stuck at the county fair?"

"No." Virginia frowned. "I don't remember that. Do you, Asa?"

Willa had nearly forgotten that day, but they had been stuck at the top for nearly twenty minutes. She also remembered who was in there with her. "They weren't there, Marc," she reminded him softly.

"Oh, that's right."

"Neither one of us was there?" Asa frowned. "You two hung out without us?"

"Sometimes," Willa admitted. "You two can be pains in the ass."

"Hey!" the twins said at the same moment.

Virginia looked at them once again, her eyes lingering on Marc's hand that hadn't left her arm, and his fingers that were still stroking her skin. "You sure there's nothing going on? We'd be cool with it if there was."

"I was in love with Willa in high school," he told them. "I'm not afraid to admit it. Don't you still have a soft spot for your first love?"

"First love?" Asa shook his head. "You never told me that."

"You never asked." He shrugged. "But if we were a couple now we would tell you. There's no reason to hide it."

"That's true," Virginia agreed, but she still looked suspicious. "Come sit with us. I think they are just about done setting up."

He had told them he had been in love with her like it was no big deal, like he didn't care if the whole world knew. It was so different from the way he acted in high school, Willa almost couldn't get her head around it. She glanced up at him as they drove back to the resort. Before, he sat with Asa; now he was sitting next to her once again, giving her no space, the warmth of his hard body seeping into her cold skin. He would feel nice on a winter's night, she thought. She could almost feel him in her bed, heating her up when it was bitterly cold outside.

"What are you thinking about, Wil?" He caught her staring.

"Nothing." She shook her head and looked away.

"Liar." He tenderly brushed his knuckles beneath her chin. "But you don't have to tell me if you don't want to."

She wanted lean into his touch, but she resisted. He was sucking her in again, and she was having a hard time resisting. She thought she was stronger than that. "That's good, because I'm not going to tell you what I'm thinking."

"I can live with that," he said softly, kissing her just beneath her ear in the spot that always made her tremble.

"This is why people think there is something going on between us."

"I don't care what anybody else thinks."

"You don't? You certainly did before."

He sat up, moving slightly away from her. She felt him stiffen and immediately she felt bad for the shot she had taken. She was about to say something, but the van stopped and let them off in front of the main lodge.

They got out without saying anything else to each other. He spoke to everyone else, though. Smiling, saying his goodbyes, making plans for the next day. She stood by watching him, and for some reason feeling bad about what she had said to him. She wasn't sure why she felt guilty. It was true that he had cared what everybody else thought when they were in high school. It was true that he put all others' feelings before hers. He had hurt her.

He's different now.

But you don't need to fall in love with him again.

She walked up to him just as he was finished saying goodbye to Asa.

"Walk me back," she said when he turned around.

He looked at her for a long moment. She couldn't read his face. "I'm sorry, Willa. Lord knows how sorry I am, but I can't apologize to you anymore. Especially since it doesn't seem to make a damn bit of difference."

"Walk me back," she said again, but this time she reached out and slipped her hand into his. "Walk me back and let me be mean to you some more."

He sighed, gently squeezing her fingers. "Okay, be mean to me. I guess I have it coming."

"You should be used to people being mean," she said to him as they started to walk. "You work in DC. I don't think a nice thing has been said about anyone there since the dawn of time."

"People are usually too scared of me to be mean."

"Scared of you?" She frowned. "You are a big guy, but nothing about you is scary. If you tell anybody this, I'll kill you, but I think you're sweet."

"Yeah, don't go spreading that shit around. It will kill my reputation."

"Why are people scared of you?"

"I'm quiet when I work. People don't know how to interpret my silence and see it as a dark side. But the truth is that I'm quiet because I hate what some of my clients do, and if I told them how really felt I would never work in that town again. I'm not supposed to pass judgment. I'm supposed to remain neutral."

"Why do you stay if you hate it? I understand why you got into it, but now you have other choices."

"I stay for the money. I make a lot of it. Sometimes I want to leave so much my gut hurts. But then I remember how poor I was growing up. We slept in a car for a year. The thought of possibly going back to that scares me. Plus, starting over isn't easy."

"I did it. I started over," she said as they approached their bungalows.

"I know. That is one of the many reasons you are better than me." He grinned at her, looking at her in that way that only he could, making her feel shy and special and pretty all in one moment. It had been a long day and the tiredness was starting to seep into her bones, but she didn't want it to be over yet.

She leaned closer to him, placing both hands on his chest as she leaned up to kiss him. She had only meant to kiss him lightly, but he stepped closer, cupped her face in his hands, and opened his mouth over hers and slid his tongue deep inside her mouth. She gripped his jacket tightly; the kiss made her dizzy, made her feel like she was falling, so she held on to him. If she was going to fall she wanted him to come with her.

"Oh God, Willa." He broke the kiss, breathing heavily he dragged his lips across her cheeks and chin and the bridge of her nose. "I don't know what it is about you, but I can't get enough."

"Come inside." Her eyes were still closed, still savoring that kiss.

"What?"

"Come inside." She didn't want to spend the night alone. She didn't want to spend the night thinking about him while her body craved his touch. She had gone too long without sex, without being made love to. Some of her best memories had been with him, and she wanted to add this night to them.

He looked at her for a long moment, studying her face as if to see if she was serious.

She closed the distance between them, sliding her hands under his shirt so she could feel the smooth, skin of his back. Setting her mouth against his, she licked across his lips asking to be let in. He groaned and before she could think, she felt her back against the door and his hands beneath her dress touching the backs of her thighs. "Are you sure about this?" he asked her, and she had never seen him more serious.

"I've never had to invite a guy in more than once. They usually take me up on my first offer."

"You asked me if I had a girlfriend, but I forgot to ask you if there is a man in your life."

"Yeah." She nodded. "He's got his hands up my dress as we speak."

He flashed her a wicked, sexy smile. "Open the door,

Willa. If you don't, you risk me stripping you naked right here."

"I might like that," she said, but turned away to unlock the door.

She barely got through the door before Marc was kissing her again, but this time it wasn't her mouth that got the special treatment. He untied the halter that kept her short dress up, lifted her hair and fluttered slow, hot kisses across her neck.

"I have wanted to do this all evening," he said between kisses. "You can't wear dresses like this and expect me to keep my sanity. All night I kept thinking about pulling on this and unwrapping you like a present."

He tugged down her dress, revealing her black strapless bra, and ran his fingers gently over the tops of her breasts. He was taking his time with her, seducing her. He didn't have to. She had been seduced by him long ago. "Take it off," she ordered. Her nipples were straining against the fabric. Her skin beneath her clothing had grown too hot. She wanted to be naked; she wanted to feel his hands and lips and breath all over her body.

"Take what off?" He tugged her dress down just a little farther until it fell to her hips. He went to his knees then, giving her a hot, wet openmouthed kiss on the small of her back. That kiss literally stole her breath, causing the throb between her legs to grow painful.

"Marc…" She tried to speak but couldn't manage more than his name. He pulled at her dress one last time, till it fell to her feet. He turned her around, and for a moment he just looked up at her.

"Stop looking at me like that." She shut her eyes, unable to take his inspection.

"Like what?" He kissed the curve of her belly, and for once in her life she felt perfect. She didn't worry that her thighs were too big or her stomach wasn't that flat. She didn't feel awkward or weird. She felt like she had only felt with him, and it made her heart hurt.

"Like you're looking at me," she said, swallowing hard as he pulled down her panties just a bit to kiss her hip. "I don't need to fall in love with you and you don't need to fall in love with me. This is just a fling."

"What?" He took his lips completely off her body and suddenly her thoughts became a little clearer.

"A fling. Isn't that what people have when they're on vacation in tropical places?"

A fling?

That was the last thing Marc was thinking about when he had followed her inside tonight.

A fling meant insignificant and fleeting. It meant that there were no feelings attached. Normally he would have welcomed that. No plans for the future. No messy break-ups. Just the two of them in the moment. But somehow having just that with Willa didn't sit well with him.

Having a fling with your first love seemed impossible.

"What if I told you I didn't want that?"

She looked down at him, clad only in her black underwear with her pouty lips parted slightly. Her eyes grew thoughtful and then she said, "But I want you, Marc." She knelt before him, slowly reaching for the buttons on his shirt. "I want this."

Every look Willa gave him, every sound she made when he touched her aroused him, but her words made him so hard he couldn't see straight.

She finished with the buttons on his shirt and pushed it all the way open, revealing his chest. She smoothed her hands over his chest. "I couldn't do this with anybody else," she told him, and she pushed his jacket and shirt down his arms. "I feel safe with you."

She inched closer and ran her tongue lightly along his lips. He grabbed her by the waist, needing to feel her, but he stopped there, too curious to see what she was going to do next.

She kissed him again as her hand wandered down his body to his pants. She unzipped him, slid her hand inside and just held him for a moment, running her thumb up his shaft. "I need this."

"It's not detachable."

She looked up at him and grinned, reminding him of that girl he once fell in love with. "I like the attachments." She wrapped her hand completely around him, stroking his entire length.

He hissed out a breath, the pleasure was so good. "I think you should stop that."

"I think you should finish undressing me." She stroked him again, every touch bringing him closer to the edge.

He grabbed her hands and pulled them above her head. "Stay like that," he ordered. He needed a moment away from her touch. She was clouding his head. He already knew that one night wouldn't be enough. One fling wouldn't satisfy him. It might be enough for her. She might be able to go back home and get on with her life, but he couldn't. She would stay with him. He would carry her with him. And knowing that he wouldn't be able to repeat this night again would drive him insane.

She reached behind her and undid the clasp of her bra with one hand. Her breasts were exposed. Round. Soft. Beautiful. She looked him in the eye and cupped them in her hands, rubbing her thumbs over her nipples.

That drove him over the edge. He got to his feet and scooped her into his arms, carrying her to her bedroom.

She landed on the bed with a bounce and he stood back as he stripped off his pants and shoes, enjoying how she looked spread on the bed nearly naked. Just a pair of black satin panties and her pretty strappy shoes.

"I thought I told you to stay put." He settled himself between her legs and pinned her arms behind her head. He took one of her breasts in his hand and gently squeezed it before he set his mouth to it. Her back arched off the bed.

"You don't listen, Willa, and that's a problem." He kissed the line down to her belly button, stopping to lick inside.

"You were…" She moaned again. "You were taking too long."

"I like to look at you." He pulled her underwear down, not all the way, but just enough to kiss the skin that was hidden there. "You should have just let me look at you. Now you are going to pay." He liked to take his time with her, even though he was on the verge of losing control. She was the kind of woman that needed to be savored, and if he was only going to have these few days with her he wanted to make sure he remembered every moment of them.

"Marc, please. I'm sorry."

He pulled her underwear all the way off, kissing the lips between her legs. She was more than ready for him, but he hadn't had his fill yet. He gently parted her, slipping one finger inside her. She grabbed his wrist, preventing him from moving.

"I'm too close. I want all of you." He relented, the need to be inside her overwhelming him.

His chest met hers and he wrapped her thighs around him. Finally they were face-to-face, pressed together with no clothes between them. It's what he had been thinking about since he had first laid eyes on her again.

She took his face in her hands and kissed him, and just as he was about to slip inside her she cursed.

"What?" He lifted his head to look at her, but the sight of her kiss-swollen lips distracted him.

"I think we should use a condom."

"Okay." He kissed her mouth, glad that she was smart enough to remember. He quickly left her to retrieve his pants.

"You have some?"

"Yeah." He pulled them out and showed her.

"You just happened to have condoms on you?" she asked as she placed her hands behind her head. "You always bring them along? You expect to get lucky everywhere you go?"

"No. I bought them in the gift shop when you went to take a nap." He handed one to her. "Put it on for me."

She sat up and did as he asked. "You were that sure I was going to sleep with you?"

"No, I heard Carlos's mother is single and thought she was pretty hot for a sixty-seven-year-old woman."

She paused for a moment, looking up at him with a frown. "Damn, she looks good for her age."

"I wasn't sure, Willa." He kissed her shoulder. "I just know that I can't be around you and not want to be with you."

"I feel the same way about you, Marc." She pulled him down on the bed, their bodies lined up, their skin touching, and she was looking at him the way she used to. She was looking at him the way she did when he knew she loved him. "Stay with me."

Chapter 6

Willa woke up the next morning as soon as Marc rolled away from her. She had slept last night wrapped in his arms, his face buried in her neck. They had never slept together before. When they were teenagers they would steal moments alone, plan out their time together. She had never been with just him. This week they had spent more uninterrupted time together than they had their entire relationship. She kind of liked it. She liked him.

He got out of bed still naked, his large, sculpted body beautiful. She watched him, her eyes drinking him in as he stretched. He had the perfect behind, and images of last night flooded her head. She had never had sex like that. Sex that made her feel like liquid afterward. Sex that left her feeling utterly and completely satisfied. Sex that made her feel so connected.

She had been in a long-term relationship with a professor. She had liked him; he was smart and funny and good on paper, but he never made her feel the way Marc did. It might have been because she hadn't been in love with him. She broke up with him when she stopped convincing herself she was.

"You're staring at me." He bent over to retrieve his pants.

"Your ass is amazing. I might have to get a picture of it before you leave."

"You like it?" He turned around and she could see his erection forming. Her heart pounded a little faster as he crawled back into bed and pushed the hair out of her face.

"Are you leaving?"

He kissed down the column of her throat. "Do you want me to?" His hand cupped her breast, stroking her nipple until it was a hard little point.

She thought about being coy, about giving him a smart-mouth answer, but all she said was, "No."

"Good." His lips touched hers, giving her a long, deep kiss that made her insides flutter. "Because I don't want to go."

"You were reaching for your pants. You don't have to stay."

"I was looking for this." He showed her the gold foil packet in his hand.

"Judging by what's going on between your legs, we're going to need that."

"You do that to me." Marc kissed her once again, one of those slow pecks that she was growing to love again. He lifted his head and looked down at her. "I don't want this to be over yet. I don't think I can get enough of you."

If she were naive she might think he was talking about more than this week, that he was talking about a future with her, but she knew that was silly. After they left this beautiful place, he would go back to his life and she would go back to hers. "It's not over yet. We have the rest of the week."

He nodded. "Two more full days." She could have sworn she saw disappointment in his eyes, but she was sure her mind was playing tricks on her.

"Maybe I could go to your bungalow tonight and we could test out that bed?"

"Yeah." He wrapped one of her curls around his finger. "We could do that."

"Don't sound so excited about it. You're likely to have a heart attack."

He grinned at her, kissing the tip of her nose. "I was just thinking about all the things I would like to do to you in the next few days. I don't think I'm going to have enough time to get everything accomplished."

"I guess you're going to have to prioritize."

He bent to kiss her chest, right where her heart was beating. "I guess we are just going to have to start right here with breakfast."

"Breakfast? What are we going to eat?"

"I don't know what you're going to have, but I'm getting ready to have some of you."

"No scuba diving for you today?" Asa asked Willa as she lay next to him on the beach late that afternoon.

"No. I'm a little too afraid of a malfunctioning oxygen tank. You know I killed somebody off that way in my second novel."

"You're paranoid, aren't you?" He grinned.

"A little bit. I went whale watching this morning with Carlos's sisters and I kept thinking about all the ways people could die at this resort. Whale watching is a good one. What if the boat never came back and the killer faked their own death on the boat so they could commit murder un-detected?"

"You're sick."

"I'm not. I worked in forensic pathology for years. You would be amazed at the many ways people die."

"No, I'm not amazed. I'm a paramedic. I like my people living."

"Me, too," she agreed. "Dead people are no fun in real life."

A boat pulled up onto the shore on the almost-deserted beach. She watched Marc emerge first. He had gone with Virginia, Carlos and Carlos's newly arrived best friend. They had gone their separate ways after spending the morning in her bed. She hadn't wanted to. If it had been her choice they would have stayed there all day. But they both knew they couldn't. They both knew they were there for Virginia, to celebrate for her.

Still, she had missed him, and not just the sex, either. She liked being around him and talking to him, and feeling him near her. That wasn't supposed to happen. She was still supposed to hate him. She was just supposed to be enjoying his body and the way he made her feel. She wasn't supposed to like him so much, to feel that soft ache when he was away from her. They had just spent five hours apart. They were going to spend the rest of their lives apart, and if she had missed him now, how was it going to be when she went back to New York?

Marc trudged up the sand and collapsed right on top of her. She smiled when she felt his still-damp body make contact with hers.

"Did you have fun?" she asked him, rubbing her hand over his bald head.

"Saw some fish. Saw a huge manta ray. Then saw my life flash before my eyes. I'm exhausted, but it was amazing." He looked right into her eyes. "I wish you were there with me to see it."

She felt that stupid tuggy feeling in her chest again, the same one she felt when she was seventeen years old and first falling in love with him.

"What about me?" Asa asked, breaking the moment. "You don't wish I was there, too?"

Marc lifted his head to look at his best friend. "When you look this good in a bathing suit I'll wish you were with me, too." He rested his head on her chest and she couldn't help but to stroke his sleepy face. She knew Asa was watching. She knew everybody thought they were together, and she couldn't keep denying things, especially when he was touching her like this. "Did you have fun whale watching?"

"Yes. Asa and I were just talking about it. I'm pretty sure my next novel is going to be about a woman who fakes her death on a whale watching trip."

"Yes, and you could have her stalk her husband before she kills him. He would think it was her but no one believes him," Marc said.

"Yes, and it would slowly drive him to madness, but instead of her killing him, she drives him to kill himself. It's got to be in some kind of grand fashion, too."

"She needs a good motive. I always kind of feel sorry for your murderers."

"Me, too. It shows you that almost anybody can be pushed to kill."

"You guys are crazy!" Asa sat up. "Both of you. If you two aren't together you should be, because both of you are certifiable."

"We're plotting. Stop being dramatic."

"Yeah, you're plotting someone's death."

"It's not a real person, Asa," Marc said. "Dr. Arthur

here writes some really good stuff. Get your head out of your ass and read."

"I did. The first book creeped me out, Wil. It made me wonder what went wrong in your childhood."

"Nothing went wrong!"

"Excuse me?" One of the hotel's staff came up to them with a note in his hand. "Mr. Simpson?"

"Yes?" Marc lifted his head, looking at the man with suspicion.

"You have a message. I was told to tell you that it was an urgent matter that couldn't wait."

Marc sat up, taking the paper from the man. "It's work. I have to respond to this. I might be a while."

He left with the man and Willa didn't see him until the next day.

"I want you to be my maid of honor," Virginia said to Willa the next afternoon. They were in Virginia's luxurious cabin, which was high in the trees and looked like a magical tree house.

"What?" The request took her by surprise. The wedding was the next night. She and Carlos were having such a small ceremony, Willa didn't think that they would do any of the traditional things.

"I've known you since I was six. How could I not have you by my side when I get married? We planned our imaginary weddings together."

"Yes, but I was the one who was supposed to marry the professional athlete, not you."

Virginia grinned happily at her. "Yeah, it's funny how things work out. The last person I'd ever thought I'd end up with is the only person I ever want to be with."

Her mind unwillingly turned to Marc, whom she hadn't seen since he left the beach the day before. She knew he was fine, that he must be working, but she had missed him last night, unable to sleep because she was waiting for his knock on her door. She had started this trip hating him, but things had changed so quickly. "When did you know he was the one?"

"When being without him became too hard and the only way I felt balanced was knowing I would be with him."

"I found you." Marc walked in then, looking rumpled and exhausted. Her heart sped up at the sight of him. "No one knew where you were. I was getting worried."

She left her seat, her feet moving toward him, her mind almost completely blank except for thoughts of him. She wrapped her arms around him, burying her face in the crook of his neck. His five-o'clock shadow scraped her skin, but she didn't care. "What do you mean you were worried about me? I haven't seen you in twenty-four hours and now you show up here all rumpled. I was starting to think those organ snatchers you had spoken about when we first arrived finally got to you."

"My organs are intact," he said, brushing a kiss across her forehead. "It's my soul you should worry about."

"What happened?"

"Sex scandal. Hookers. Three of them. Mr. Morality and Values got caught with them in his car. They want us to spin it as if he were counseling them. I'm not sure how the public is going to buy that when nobody was wearing pants, but we'll make it work."

"Is it always like this?"

"Yes."

"Why do you do it? You work with people you don't like. You stand up for things you don't believe in."

"It's my job. What do you expect me to do?"

"Something you like. Something that makes you happy. This doesn't make you happy. You're in the most beautiful place on the planet with people who love you and you let your job get in the way of that. Why do you always let things get in the way of people you love?"

"We're not just talking about my job anymore, are we?"

"We are talking about your job. We are here for five days to celebrate Gin's wedding and you have gone missing for twenty-four hours without a word to any of us."

"You're mad at me."

"You're damn right I'm mad at you."

"Why?" He slid his hands up her arms, narrowing his eyes at her. "Why are you so mad at me?"

"Because you weren't here. Because we only have these five days together," she said. But as soon as the words flew out of her mouth, she wished she could suck them back in.

"Whoa," she heard Virginia say from behind her and she remembered her best friend was there. She turned to look at her, lost for words. "If you tell me there's nothing going on between you now, I'll smack you."

"Okay. Maybe there's a little something going on," Willa admitted, "but it didn't happen until after we had dinner on the beach."

Virginia threw up her arms in frustration. "That's the first thing that should have come out of your mouth when I saw you this morning."

"Yell at her later. I need to steal her for a few minutes. Let's go, Dr. Arthur." Marc looked at her with triumph in his eyes. And before she could protest he was pulling her out of the room.

"Where are you taking me?" He didn't answer, just kept tugging her away from Virginia's bungalow, but he didn't take her to one of the paved paths that led back to the center of the resort. He took her into the thick trees that surrounded them. "Marc!"

He stopped abruptly, pushing her against the nearest

tree. She should have smacked him, but she couldn't deny the excitement that spiked inside her when she saw the look in his eyes. Desire. He wanted her. He stepped closer, sliding his hands over her waist, not giving her a moment to take in a breath before he kissed her hard. His hands were all over her. She felt them hot on her skin, under her dress, cupping the backs of her thighs. She felt his mouth, too, hard, insistent, wet. If he weren't holding her so tightly against him she would have slumped over. Her body couldn't support itself, couldn't stand on its own. All it could do was experience him and his touch and the thousands of feelings that were running through her.

He broke the kiss, but only so he could set his lips on her neck, kissing her in the spot he knew made her go weak. "What are you doing?"

"Baby, if you don't know—" he slid his large hand further up the back of her thigh to her behind, where he cupped her cheek "—I'm about to make it crystal clear."

"You're trying to get into my pants," she moaned as he kissed her throat. "But I'm mad at you. How does that turn you on?"

"You're mad at me for not being around for the last twenty-four hours."

"Yeah, only I didn't realize I was mad until you came back."

He gifted her with a beautiful smile and then captured her lower lip between his teeth, giving it a playful tug before he slid his tongue deep inside her mouth. She almost got caught up, lost in him again, but she pulled away.

"Why does that make you happy?"

"Why are you so mad? You said this was just a fling."

"Well, just because this is just a fling doesn't mean I wasn't waiting to hear from you all day. It doesn't mean that I didn't wait up all night for you to knock on my door. It doesn't mean I didn't miss you!"

"I missed you, too," he said softly. "I had to go into town yesterday because the resort doesn't have video conferencing. I didn't get finished with that mess until 2:00 a.m. I wanted to come by to see you but I didn't want to wake you, and I didn't want you to think I was coming over just to have sex. Then I was on the phone all morning with my boss trying to come up with a plan, but I could barely focus because I was thinking about the next time I would see you. The fact that you missed me, the fact that you want to spend as much time with me as I want to spend with you, tells me that you have feelings for me."

"What?" She tried to pull away from him. "Don't be ridiculous."

"It's not ridiculous. I have feelings for you, too. When I look at you, when I hear your voice, when I see you smile, it reminds me that you're not just some girl I dated. You were someone I loved, and no matter how hard I tried, no matter how many women I've dated, I can't seem to get you out of my mind."

She stood there stunned by his admission, her heart pounding against her rib cage. Yes, she had missed him. Yes, he made her feel heady and happy, and beautiful and wanted. But it was nothing. And if it were, it could easily be blamed on the setting and nostalgia and a slew of other things she couldn't explain. It wasn't real. She would go back to her life and he would go back to his, and those feelings would fade. Life would go back to normal and he would be just another pleasant memory.

She didn't want to fall in love.

She liked her single-girl lifestyle.

She liked not missing anyone.

She liked being in her head all day.

"Willa." He whispered her name as he brushed his lips across her cheek, bringing her out of her thoughts. "Say something."

She looked up at him. Into his beautiful expressive eyes, and realized that in that moment, she didn't want to be in her head. She didn't want to be alone with her thoughts. She only wanted him.

"Take me back to your place."

She didn't remember the journey back to the bungalow. All she could remember was being breathless, feeling her heart pounding and the blood rushing through her ears. He led her inside, closing the door behind her. They stood there for a moment, silently staring at each other. She still didn't know what to say to him, how to respond to his beautiful words, so she stepped forward and kissed him, wrapped her arms around him, saying with her mouth what her words couldn't. "Make love to me," she managed to get out in the brief moment their lips separated.

"Bedroom."

"Too far. Can't wait." She unzipped his pants, reaching her hand inside to stroke him. He cursed, shoving up her dress so he could tear at her underwear. She became frantic then, ripping at the buttons on his shirt so she could feel his skin. She was just smoothing her hands over his chest as he leaned her against the wall and put a condom on and pushed inside her.

She was ready for him; the throbbing between her legs was so intense it was nearly painful. He didn't go slow this time; there were no gentle long strokes. His pace was quick and hard. It was too much and not enough at the same time. She pushed back against him, meeting him stroke for stroke, crying out his name, saying words she couldn't remember.

"I can't hold on much longer. You've got to come for me, Willa."

"I'm just waiting for you."

He paused for a moment, looking at her with such intensity it made her tremble. He kissed her again, sealing his mouth to hers as he pumped hard inside her. Climax hit hard then and he let go, too, calling her name. She felt dazed and breathless and tingly. No coherent thoughts ran through her mind. She just felt satisfied and warm and for the first time in a long time, she felt happy.

It was one of those moments Marc wished didn't have to end. Willa was wrapped around him, her lips on his throat, her hair brushing against his chin. He felt like that little thing that had been missing from his life was finally there. But he knew they couldn't stay like that, with him still inside her and her pushed up against the wall. It was one of the few times he had completely lost control with a woman, wanting her so bad that it didn't matter where they were.

"That was…" Willa looked up at him with a lavish grin. "That was something."

"Something?" He smiled back at her, then led her away from the wall and to his bedroom, finally feeling a little bit of balance in his unbalanced world. He hadn't lied to her when he told her focusing on work was hard because thoughts of her kept popping into his mind. Thoughts of him undressing her, thoughts of her pretty lips pressed against his, thoughts of him waking up beside her. His boss wanted him to fly back last night, to be there when the senator gave his press conference, but he refused. Virginia had been a very good friend to him all these years and he didn't want to disappoint her. But more than that, he didn't want to leave Costa Rica, because he didn't want to leave Willa. And he knew if he flew home yesterday he might not ever see her again.

It was a risk he couldn't take.

They were both still dressed and she stood before him, like a present that needed to be unwrapped. He could have just lifted the dress up over her head, but that would have been too quick, so he slid the straps down her arms, revealing her slowly. Her bra was baby-doll pink today and so sexy against her pretty brown skin. He couldn't help but to kiss her collarbone, the top of her cleavage, her beating heart.

"You really like to take your time undressing me, don't you?"

"You're sexy," he said, smoothing his hands over her hips as her dress hit the floor. "I can't wait till winter. Just thinking of peeling you out of extra clothing makes my mouth water."

She looked up at him in surprise, her mouth dropping open as if she was going to say something, but she didn't. She just leaned forward and kissed his cheek.

"I ripped your underwear." He kissed her neck as he unhooked her bra.

"That's okay." She shut her eyes and tilted her head back to give him further access to her neck. "I think every woman needs to have a beautiful man tear her clothes at least once."

"You think I'm beautiful?" He slipped her ripped underwear off her body and then knelt before her to take off her shoes.

"I'm a woman of discerning tastes. You don't actually think I would sleep with somebody ugly."

He gently pushed her onto the bed. "That's not true. I saw a picture of your last boyfriend."

She gasped. "He had inner beauty. I didn't mind that

he wore braces at thirty and was a little shorter than me. How did you see my last boyfriend, anyway?"

He stripped off his clothes, past ready to feel her nude body against his. She watched his movements with a little spark in her eye and it managed to turn him on even more. "I work in DC. I had him checked out."

"You didn't!"

"I didn't. Virginia showed me a picture of you two at Comic-Con on her phone. I didn't know you were into that stuff."

"I'm not. I was being supportive. Why did Gin show you my picture?"

"Because I asked about you." He climbed into bed beside her, pulling her close, wrapping his arms around her. "She told me she wished you'd stop dating dweebs."

"I hadn't realized you two were so close."

"Asa and Gin are family to me. I spend a lot of holidays with them. I always hoped I would run into you when I was there, but since your folks moved south you don't spend time in Jersey anymore."

"No. It makes me sad. Even though I was a little bit of an outcast, I loved growing up there."

"I did, too. I was mad as hell at first that my mother sent me there, but I ended up loving it. Being there shaped the man I became."

"You gave up football," she said absently as she rested her head on his chest. "Are you happy you did? Are you happy with the way your life turned out?"

"I didn't love football as much as you think. I've had a good life."

"But are you happy?"

He smoothed her curls out of her face, looking into her wide brown eyes. "Right now I am."

"I want you to be happy, Marc." She climbed on top of

him, straddling his forming erection, and bent to kiss his chest. "This feels good, doesn't it?"

"Us?" He pulled her down to kiss her lips. "It does. It feels really good." She rubbed against him, causing him to go fully erect.

He kissed her slowly. "I'll be good to you this time. Wil, I won't hurt you again."

"Hurt me again? What are you talking about?"

"Things will be crazy the next few weeks at work, but I want you to come down to DC and spend some time with me."

She looked shocked, but he couldn't understand why she was so surprised by his request. He knew she had feelings for him. He could see it in the way she looked at him and feel it in the way she touched him. They had something special before and he threw it away. He wasn't going to make that mistake twice. "Marc…"

"This is good, Willa. Me and you are good together. I haven't felt like this with anybody else, and you can't look me in the eye and tell me it's not the same for you."

She looked helpless for a moment. "Of course this feels good. Of course no one else has ever made me feel the way you do. There is no other you. You were my first love and part of me is always going to love you. But this was never supposed to be permanent, or lasting. This was just supposed to be…" She shook her head, clearly flustered. "I don't know what it was supposed to be, but I have my life in New York and you have yours in Washington. And we're here in paradise and everything feels different and romantic and perfect, but who's to say things will stay like that? Your work takes you away for days, and I write. And I wear sweats and don't comb my hair for days while I'm on a deadline. I'll be in my head. And I'll ignore you. Things won't be perfect then. We won't be in paradise and we won't feel the same way. And I want to leave here feeling this way, remembering how happy I was with you this week."

"You're so convinced that we are going to fail that you aren't even willing to try."

Her eyes filled with tears. "I loved you so much, but we were kids then. And our lives are totally different. We had a good week. It won't be this good when we go back to real life. You probably won't even think about me when you're back in DC."

"Damn it, Wil, I haven't ever stopped thinking about you. You don't get to tell me what's going on in my head."

"You'll try. We'll both try, but it won't work and I can't get over you twice. Please, don't ask me to." She kissed him slowly, softly, and he could feel her love in this kiss. She didn't have to tell him because he already knew, but he was so damn mad at her for not wanting to try. "Kiss me." She opened her eyes to look at him. "Kiss me back."

He didn't want to. She wouldn't meet him halfway. Every relationship he had, every woman he was with, he had compared to her. He couldn't recapture the feelings he had with her and knew he never would be able to.

"Marcus, please." She kissed him again, more deeply if that was possible. "Kiss me back. Make me feel good. Love me one more time." He broke, then.

Love her one more time? He had never stopped. He would never stop loving her.

Chapter 7

He had made love to her twice more that night and again in the morning. It was different than the other times they were together. It was still bone melting and satisfying, but there was almost an urgency to it. Or maybe it was just her. Maybe because she knew that tomorrow she going back to New York and leaving paradise, leaving him behind for good. She wanted to say yes to him. She wanted to throw caution to the wind and jump feetfirst back into love with him.

We could make it work, she thought. It didn't matter that she hadn't seen him in fourteen years. It hadn't mattered that she didn't really know him anymore or that they had just been together for just a few days, because it felt amazing.

But it did matter. She just wanted a fling, a few days where she could let down her hair and be somebody she normally wasn't. A few days when she wasn't on a deadline and spending more time thinking about her characters' lives than her own. And she had achieved that. She made some good memories, too. She shouldn't feel this much sadness about it ending, only a bittersweetness. But she was sad. She had hurt him.

She could see it in his face. Hear it in the few words he had spoken to her. He was feeling nostalgic, reliving old times. He had to know that they couldn't work. He was sexy and successful. He was a good man, and she knew he probably had to beat women off with a stick. He would be all right. He would go back to his life and forget about her.

It was for the best.

She walked up to the site of Virginia's ceremony and gasped. It was being held in the butterfly garden. When she heard where it was going to take place she thought little of the name. But there were butterflies everywhere. Perched on flowers and in the trees, the colorful beauties took the place of decorations. Anything man-made couldn't live up to these natural ornaments.

"It's pretty amazing, right?" Virginia said. She saw her best friend standing just inside one of the little huts outlining the property. Willa's eyes filled with tears seeing her. She wore a simple silk gown that fit the setting and her toned body perfectly. But it was the flowers in her loose hair and the glowing look on her face that truly made her beautiful that day.

"I didn't think it was possible to be this happy for someone else." She rushed over to her and hugged her tightly. "But I'm so happy for you."

"Don't you start crying! I've been trying not to cry all day. You look gorgeous, by the way. I keep meaning to tell you that. I've never seen you look so amazing."

"Ha!" She swiped at her tears. "When I'm at home I live in yoga pants and baggy T-shirts. I only look this good for you. And anyway, I'm supposed to be telling you how perfect you look. This place is amazing. I'm so glad to be a part of it all."

"I knew it was something special when I saw it. I'm supposed to be in the bridal suite but I wanted to see people's faces when they walked in."

"They'll be talking about this wedding for the rest of their lives."

"You better start planning now if you're going to top me. How much do you think it'll cost to rent out the Met?"

"I'm not getting married anytime soon," she said softly, feeling sadness she hadn't expected.

"I know you and Marc just started dating, but he's in love with you, Willa. It's going to happen soon."

"We're not dating," she said a little too quickly.

"What? But yesterday… He dragged you away and no one saw either of you for the rest of the night."

"I was with him, but we're friends. We're going to stay friends."

"But Willa! You love him. I see it."

"We're familiar strangers. Five days together after fourteen years apart is not the basis for long-term relationship."

"Maybe not, but you have to see him again. You have to try."

"This is your day. Let's focus on you."

"I know we haven't been as close as we should these past couple of years, but I love you. You're my best friend and I want you to be happy. Marcus Simpson will make you happy."

"Marc and I had a thing once and he broke my heart, okay? So excuse me if I'm not ready to plan my wedding."

"You're scared," she accused her. "You've been scared of being hurt for years, and that's why you only date men who you could never fall in love with."

"And I'm going to die a lonely spinster with my thirteen cats," Willa said, but she knew her friend was right. She wasn't scared of him hurting her again. She had grown up. She was more confident. She knew what she had to offer the world. But she was afraid of losing herself in him. Afraid of taking a backseat to his needs. Afraid of losing that thing that made her a great writer. "We are done talking about this." She shook her head. "Let's talk about your honeymoon, or potential baby names, or the price of butter these days."

"Fine." Virginia rolled her eyes. "But when I get back from Europe we are going to have a nice long chat whether you want to or not. We're moving to New York. I'll be teaching a painting class there and you won't be able to avoid me."

"You're moving back?" Willa was happy to hear it, happy to have her friends closer. She was going to need them.

"Yes, for a while. Now let's get to the bridal suite before I get caught. I'm getting married in an hour, and I'm freaking out a little."

"I never realized how much I loved you until I spent time without you," Marc heard Virginia say in her vows to Carlos. "And when we were apart I realized how incomplete my life was without you in it."

He knew he should have been focusing on Virginia and how moving the ceremony was, but he couldn't help but look over to Willa. She wore a bright turquoise dress and a spray of white flowers in her hair. She was teary-eyed and beaming at her best friend. *Beautiful* wasn't a strong enough word to describe her. It almost hurt to look at her. Hurt because he knew that in a few hours they would be going their separate ways.

She turned around to look at him them, their eyes locking, the happiness melting off her face. Maybe it was stupid of him to try to rekindle things after fourteen years apart and only a few days in each other's company. Maybe she was right. Maybe it was the air. Maybe they would get back to their normal lives and fall out of whatever it was they were currently in. Maybe he could believe that if he hadn't ever been in love with her in the first place.

"Are you going to come clean about what's going on between you two?" Asa whispered as he turned his attention back to the ceremony.

"I love her, but she doesn't want to give us a shot."

"You're going to let that stop you, are you? Willa is the type you fight for. Fight for her. You'll hate yourself if you don't."

Asa was right. Marc was going to have to fight to keep the best thing that ever happened to him.

There were about twenty guests at the reception but Willa could focus on only one. Marc was standing in front of the waterfall with Asa, looking sexy in his gray suit and coral-colored shirt. He was chatting with one of Carlos's cousin, a beautiful woman with long dark hair that went down to her waist. Women were drawn to him. He would go home and find some gorgeous woman to love. She was sure of that. But he kept looking at her. She felt his eyes on her, and he gave her long, hot looks that made her skin tingle. It was hard chatting with the other guests, pretending to be cheerful when all she wanted to do was cross the patio to be near him.

They could have tonight. It was getting late. Guests were starting to head back to their rooms. She could sneak off with him. Her flight left early in the morning. They could spend just a few more hours together, but she knew that it would be worse if she stayed with him. Saying good-bye would be just too hard. It would cloud her. She didn't want to leave this beautiful place, but she really needed to go home. To be in her space, to get back to her routine. Then she would be able to see things clearly. Right now her vision was blurry and the only thing she could see was him.

His eyes met hers again. It must have been the hundredth time it happened that night. She couldn't take it anymore. She walked over to him after spending all evening away from him. He opened his arms to her, tucking her into his embrace, kissing the bridge of her nose. It felt natural and normal and right. She felt like she fit there. Like she fit with him. And it wasn't the way it felt in high school. It felt bigger. It felt deeper. It was something she never expected. Something she never planned for.

"Your arms are cold. Let me give you my jacket."

"No." She reached up to kiss him, and he gave her one of those slow, soft pecks that made her melt.

"This was a mistake on your part," he said in between kisses. "If you think I'm letting you get away, you're dead wrong. This is too good to give up."

"Marc." An unfamiliar voice called his name and they both looked up to see a man in a rumpled suit before them.

"Kevin." Marc looked shocked. "What are you doing here?"

"I'm so sorry to bother you, but Mr. Connor had a massive heart attack this morning after you two spoke. He wants you by his side. He sent a private plane."

He let go of her, his face going stony.

"Who is Mr. Connor?" she asked, feeling him slip away already.

"My boss," he said distractedly. "How bad is it?" he asked his colleague.

"We're not sure he's going to make it. We need you to come back. You're second-in-command."

He nodded, taking a step away from her, before he paused and turned to look back at her. "I've got to go, Willa. I'm sorry."

Of course he did. This was his livelihood. A job he worked so hard at to get to the top. It came first. Something always came first for him, and it wasn't going to be her. "Go. I'll tell Virginia why you had to leave."

"I'm sorry."

"Don't be. I should have expected it. This is your life."

"Willa…"

"Goodbye, Marc." She walked away from him, realizing she had been right all along.

Chapter 8

It had been three weeks since Willa left Costa Rica. It was supposed to be just a vacation, a time she looked back on with only pleasant memories, but those five days in paradise left a bigger mark on her than she had thought they would.

She had come home, gotten back to her life, but still thought about Marc. She was so sure that once things around her had gone back to normal, thoughts of him would fade. That she wouldn't wake up in the morning wishing she felt his warm, heavy body beside her. But she had been wrong, because thoughts of him hadn't faded. If anything they grew more intrusive with each passing day. She knew it was insane. Five days together after fourteen years apart. He shouldn't have left such an imprint on her heart. There shouldn't be sadness weighing her down. Life shouldn't seem so dull without him.

But nothing made her heart race, nothing made her

excited or happy or any of the emotions that she had felt when she was with him. And for the first time she was having a hard time writing. Normally the words poured out of her. Normally she would spend hours pounding at her keyboard, only looking up when hunger got to be too much for her. But now it seemed her fingers and brain were disconnected. They wouldn't work the way they used to. It made her realize that maybe she wasn't as happy as she thought she was before. That she had been existing, but she wasn't living.

She had to switch things up. Sitting in her apartment thinking about him would do her no good. So she got dressed, not in her yoga pants that seemed to be her uniform lately, but in clothes that made her feel pretty, and she decided to walk that day. She went around her neighborhood and shopped in stores she had never been to, ate in a café that she had passed a million times and never knew it was there. There was a whole world around her that she had been ignoring, and she explored it thinking it would take her mind off him, but it didn't really. She saw couples together walking hand in hand, sharing smiles, just being happy in each other's presence. She wondered if she had taken the chance, done as he had asked and gone to Washington, if they would have been the same way.

They could have been, but then she thought about the last time she saw him and how his job had pulled him away so many times in those few days. His job would always pull him away. He was important to his firm, but she wanted to be important to him. She wanted to come first. It was selfish, she knew, but he had thrown her away before. She refused to be thrown away again. Plus he hadn't even called. She had expected him to, the next day, the next week. She jumped every time her phone rang, expecting it to be him, but it never was, and it just proved to her that she had been right all along. That their fling had been just that.

But even though things hadn't worked out with Marc she didn't regret one moment of her time with him, because he taught her that she didn't have to settle in life. That she could be with someone who made her feel, whom she could love. And she did love Marc. She had never stopped. He taught her that it was okay to risk falling in love with somebody, because the alternate was never loving at all. And not loving was dull. Not loving made the world seem gray.

She wanted a man in her life, and family, and children, she decided when she walked past the park on the way back to her building that afternoon. She was thirty years old. It was time she really let herself love again.

She pulled out her cell phone and dialed Asa's number as she rode the elevator back to her apartment. She loved him, too, but could never think of him as anything more than a brother. Being back home taught her that she needed to make an effort to keep the people she loved most in life close to her. Asa lived a cab ride away. There was no reason they shouldn't see each other.

"Hey! I hope you're calling me with good news."

"Good news?" She shook her head. "I would like to have dinner with you this week. Is that good news?"

"Oh." He sounded disappointed. "You're sure there's nothing else you wanted to tell me?"

"No. Is there something I should be telling you?"

"Where are you?"

"In the elevator going up to my apartment."

"You haven't been home yet?"

"I've been out all day. Why?"

"No reason," he said quickly. "Just call me back later. Okay?"

"Asa…"

He disconnected, leaving her confused. The elevator doors opened and she stepped out, still staring at her phone. She wondered if she should call Virginia, but she didn't want to bother her newlywed friend, especially since she hadn't been back from her honeymoon for more than a day.

"Hey, you shouldn't stare at your phone while you're walking," she heard a man say. "It can lead to an accident."

She looked ahead of her to see Marc sitting on the floor in front of her apartment. The air rushed out of her lungs as she took him in. He was dressed for the cold, late-fall day in a navy blue coat and smart-looking hat. He smiled up at her, beautiful as ever, but what she couldn't help but notice were the two large black suitcases that sat on either side of him.

"Willa, are you going to say something?" The smile dropped from his face and he looked up at her with concern touching his eyes.

Her throat started to burn and she blinked as tears started to form. "What are you doing here?" she asked as a hot tear slipped down her cheek.

He scrambled to his feet and wrapped her in a tight embrace. "I love you, Willa. That's what." He tipped her head back so he could wipe away her tears with his thumbs. "I know I shouldn't have ambushed you. I should have called and told you that I quit my job and gave up my apartment. I should have discussed with you the fact that I can't sleep at night because I think about you so much. I should have warned you that I was coming after you. I should have told you that you're it for me, that you make me laugh, and you make me think and you make me crazy and that I need for you to be my wife one day. But I thought if I showed up here with no place to live that you would get the picture."

"Marc!" She couldn't process her feelings. She couldn't think coherent thoughts. He was here. He was here and he was holding her and her heart was beating so fast she felt was going to pass out. "You quit your job?"

"I'm going back to school. I enrolled in the next term for Teachers College at Columbia. I'm going to get my master's in education. I'm going to do some consulting work here for the mayor's office, but nothing like before. My job was my life, and that shouldn't ever be how it is. I didn't want to lose you by staying in a job that made me unhappy. So I'm here. I'm here to love you."

"I—I don't know what to say." It was true. She was shocked and overwhelmed and overjoyed. He was here in front of her.

"I can get an apartment here. We can just date for a while, go slow if you want, but I'm in this for the long haul and I don't want to go slow. I want you." His eyes roamed her face. He looked so unsure, so adorable, that it made her heart melt. "I know you don't know what to say, but say something, please."

She pinched his arm. Hard.

"Ouch! What the hell?"

"What took you so long?" She grabbed his face, kissing him deeply. "I missed you."

"Starting over is hard. I had to settle some things before I left that life behind." He kissed down her jawline. "I want to marry you, Wil. Tell me you want this." He slowly stroked his hands down her back. "Tell me you're okay with me being here."

"I love you." She looked up at him. "I never really stopped, but I love the man you've become more than the boy you used to be. I don't want to take things slow. I want you to be my family."

"Good." He sighed. "Because I got this ring burning a

hole in my pocket and I'm itching to give it to someone. If you weren't going to take it I was prepared to give it to your mail lady."

"Of course I'll take it." She kissed him again. "I'll take you, too."

Epilogue

Willa eased herself from her chair and rubbed her aching back. It was only 3:00 p.m., but she was done writing for the day. Marc was due home from school any moment now and she always liked to be there to greet him. He had graduated with his teaching degree and had taken a job teaching history at an all-boys academy for at-risk students, never looking back to his old career.

Teaching was hard. He went in early most mornings and up until a few months ago, he stayed past five to plan his lessons and grade papers and tutor kids who needed his help, but Willa could see that her husband was happy.

Fulfilled.

He smiled when he talked about his students. He told her stories about boys who people thought were headed for a life of crime were now heading for Ivy League schools. His happiness was infectious.

And for the first time in her adult life Willa was happy,

too. It made Willa not want to write such dark novels anymore. She had been afraid her life was going to change
if she made a go of it with Marc. Afraid he would judge
her eating Chinese food for breakfast. Afraid she could
no longer go stay in sweats and write for fifteen hours a
day if she wanted to. But he ate Chinese food with her
and brought her steaming mugs of tea when she went on
her writing binges.

But she made sure she made time for him. Not because
she had to. Not because she was now his wife, but because
she wanted to. For the first time in a very long time she
wanted to have a real life and not experience it through
her characters. And life was truly sweet.

She made her way to the couch just as she heard Marc's
keys in the door. Her heart beat a little faster. Eighteen
months in and she still felt a rush whenever she saw him.

"Hey, sexy." He dropped his bag by the door and walked
over to her, a smile on his face and a paper bag in his hand.

"How's my favorite teacher today?"

"I'm great. I brought you a cupcake. Chocolate peanut butter."

She grinned up at him. "How did you know?"

He went down on his knees before her and kissed her
very large belly. "How did I know? I caught you dipping
leftover Halloween candy into a tub of peanut butter."

"Doctor says I should be eating green things and things
that grow in nature and don't have cartoon characters on
the packaging, but this kid wants candy bars and cereal
with enough sugar to choke a horse."

"How is my little man today?" He kissed her baby bump
a half dozen times. "Is he ready to make his grand entrance yet?"

He was so excited about their son. Sometimes Willa
thought she was going to have to fight to get to hold him.

"We still have over two weeks to my due date. But he was very well behaved today and let me get in all my writing. I finished my book."

Marc looked up at her, pride in his eyes, as he rubbed her belly in slow, loving circles. "That means he's getting ready to come. And because he's a gentleman like his father he's allowing you to finish your book before he comes."

"Because he knows that I will have to focus all my time on him."

"It would be a little inconvenient if an idea for a scene struck you while you were in the middle of labor."

"Only a little." She laughed. "Help me off of this couch, Marc?"

"Why? Is there something you need? I can get it for you."

He would get it for her. He was a good husband. A good man. He would be a good father soon. "Just help me up." He pulled her up and she stumbled into him, her belly seeming to have its own gravitational pull. She wrapped her arms around him and drew him close. "This is what I wanted." She rested her head against his strong chest. "I'm not going to have much time with you alone soon."

"We'll make time." He kissed her forehead. "You're sure about this? About the baby? About this life we have?"

"It's a little late for regrets, don't you think?"

He looked down at her, his expression serious, but with love in his eyes. "I know this isn't the life you had planned for yourself."

"No, but it's a better life than I could have imagined. My only regret is that we didn't get to live it sooner."

"I love you, Willa," he said just before he kissed her.

She would have told him that she loved him, too, if her mind hadn't gone blank due to his expert kisses.

"Come on." He took her by the hand and led her toward the bedroom. "I know a good way we can spend some good alone time together."

"And maybe bring the baby sooner?" He didn't care that she had gained fifty pounds, or that her feet grew, or that she now waddled when she walked. He always seemed to want her.

"There's nothing wrong with wanting to bring another piece of you into this world."

He loved her. Just like he promised he would, and she knew that unlike the characters in her books, she would live happily ever after.

* * * * *

REQUEST YOUR FREE BOOKS!

2 FREE NOVELS
PLUS 2 FREE GIFTS!

KIMANI
ROMANCE ™

Love's ultimate destination!

"You're all cloak and dagger." Nate nodded at the way
she held the menu in front of her face. "Unless you need
glasses.

The way she frowned was cute. The corners of her
mouth turned down and her bottom lip poked out. A
shoe made direct contact with his shin. "My eyesight is
perfect."

"Not just your eyesight." Nate cocked his head to get a
glimpse of the hourglass curve of her shape.

"Does your cheesy machismo usually work on women?"

Nate flashed a grin. "It worked on you last week." He regretted the words the second before he finished the *K* in week. Amelia's foot came into contact with his shin again. "Sorry. Chalk this up to being nervous."

Amelia settled back against the black leather booth. "You're supposed to be nervous?"

"Who wouldn't be?" Nate relaxed in his seat. "You breeze into town and drop a wad of cash on me just to make me do work for what you could have hired someone else to do, and much more cheaply, too."

The little flower in the center of her white spaghetti-strap top rose up and down. Even through the flicker of the flame bouncing off the deep maroon glass candleholder, he caught the way her cheeks turned pink.

"Let's say I don't trust anyone around town to do the work for me."

Don't miss HIS SOUTHERN SWEETHEART
by Carolyn Hector, available October 2016
wherever Harlequin® Kimani Romance™
books and ebooks are sold!